HOLY
HUSTLER

HOLY HUSTLER

A NOVEL BY

P.L. WILSON

www.urbanbooks.net

Published by Urban Books, LLC
Copyright © 2007 by P.L. Wilson

ISBN-13: 978-1-933967-70-7
ISBN-10: 1-933967-70-6
First Trade Printing February 2007
First Mass Market Printing June 2009

Printed in the United States of America

10 9 8 7 6 5 4 3 2 1

Distributed by Kensington Publishing Corp.
Submit Wholesale Orders to:
Kensington Publishing Corp.
c/o Penguin Group (USA) Inc.
Attention: Order Processing
405 Murray Hill Parkway
East Rutherford, NJ 07073-2316
Phone: 1-800-526-0275
Fax: 1-800-227-9604

Acknowledgments

Thank God almighty first and foremost. I'd like to thank my patient and wonderful mother Deborah Tucker Bodden for teaching her daughters, Denise and me, that everything worth having requires hard work. Then, my stepfather Herbert for keeping my mom happy, and Lydell R. Wilson, thanks for loving and supporting me in ways I can not fathom.

I have a list of Sheros I'd like to thank for their constant support of my work and in my life . . . Monica Hodge, Shanell Cavil, Marilyn Glazier, LaShawanda Moore, Lee Lee Baines, Tameka Brown. My love and thanks to Keywanne Hawkins and the rest of the most exquisite ladies of Sigma Gamma Rho Sorority Inc.

Reshonda Tate Billingsley, my sister in publishing . . . I hope these words attempt to express my appreciation for all of your unwavering support. Thanks for the advice, the nod when something worked, and the honesty, when it just didn't click. *I Know I've Been Changed* is a gem!

I'd like to thank my handsome little brother Irvin Kelvin Seguro, my nephews, nieces and the rest of my supportive family.

Finally, my deepest appreciation goes to Candace Cottrell for supporting this story, and of course special thanks to my favorite publisher, Mark Anthony and Sabine for believing in me and this story.

If I forgot anyone, it's only because these things can go on and on . . . but I hope you enjoy the story, feel free to drop me a line at *Sylkkep@yahoo.com*.

My sweet Payton . . . your existence mystifies me,

Your smile inspires me

until you . . .

I never knew I could love so much.

CHAPTER 1

"Ohhhh, chile, Pastor Goodlove tore up that sermon today," Michelle Goodlove commented. Her light brown eyes glowed as she spoke. Michelle's brown skin was a stark contrast to her light eyes and auburn hair.

"Umph, yeah, he did do good today, but I just can't stand the sight of that 'ole Theola," Tammy huffed. "You see her sitting up there all regal and grand, like she got some class?"

Michelle moved her glass of lemon-flavored water to the side. They sat at the bar in Pappadeaux Seafood Kitchen after service, waiting for a table and their other friend, Kim.

"Girl, *hursh* your mouth talking 'bout our first lady like that!" Michelle looked around the bustling restaurant for familiar faces. The last thing she needed was for someone to go back and tell Pastor Gee, as she called him, that she was sitting around talking about her new mother-in-law. Michelle wasn't sure she could even call Theola Goodlove that at all, considering the fact that Theola was a year younger than Michelle, who was thirty-three.

"She may be *your* first lady, but she ain't none of mine, that's for sure," Tammy insisted. "I mean, she's younger than the pastor's own son. What in the world was he thinking when he married that skank? I just think it's wrong."

"Y'all must be talking about that 'ole nasty ass' Theola," Kim said as she slid onto a bar stool, and right into the conversation. "Say what you want about her gold digging ass, but she sure was sharp today. I do have to give her that."

"Kim, girl, shame on you for cussing like a sailor and church ain't even been out a good hour," Michelle mocked.

"Well, I just believe in keeping it real," Kim said as she waved the bartender over. "Theola may be nasty, but she damn sure knows how to spend the pastor's money. Girl, did you see that new convertible BMW she pulled up in today?" Kim flipped her jet-black weave over her shoulder.

"Oh yes, chile. It was hot for sure. But y'all know Sister Carol, may God rest her soul, would've never bought such an expensive car." Tammy shook her head and sipped from her own citrus water. "Just a doggone shame is all I got to say about it."

"Y'all sound just like Mama Sadie and the holy rollers." Michelle leaned in, trying to whisper. "Apparently, Mama Sadie and her crew tried to have an intervention with Theola; you know, about her umm, questionable church attire."

"Www-hat?" Tammy leaned in closer too. "When did this happen? I ain't heard a word about this."

"Well, you didn't hear it from me, but it was last

Thursday before choir rehearsal. From what I hear, Mama Sadie began by telling Theola that Sister Carol would never have been caught dead in half the sinful things she chose to wear into the Lord's house. Mama Sadie even said that a couple of times it had been brought to her attention that Theola had the audacity to show up without wearing a slip! Then she strongly suggested that in the future, Theola's dresses should attempt to get close to her knees, if not past them, and that she should keep from exposing her shoulders and so much cleavage."

"No shit?" Kim asked. Michelle shook her head.

"Girl, you don't even know the worst of it. Apparently, Mama Sadie said chiffon, spandex, lace, and rayon were not acceptable choices when deciding what to wear to church," Michelle squealed.

Kim slapped her leg, and then sipped her Mimosa.

"Now, I don't know if this is true," Michelle continued, "but I heard Theola looked at Mama Sadie and her pack and said, 'If you old hens don't like the clothes I wear, you can always rejoice in kissing my—" Tammy grabbed Michelle's arm.

"You lyin'!" she hollered.

"What I wouldn't have paid to be a fly on the wall during that intervention," Kim said as their waitress approached.

As they were being led to their table, Michelle saw Tammy's head cocked to the side. She reached for Michelle's arm as they followed the waitress to their table.

"Um, look over there in that corner. I know that ain't Damien, as in your husband Damien, with that little hooker Jazzlyn. I heard she had to leave Wilshire Baptist for screwing one of the very married deacons over there," Tammy said as she directed Michelle's attention to the far right corner of the restaurant.

Once they arrived at their table, Tammy and Kim sat, but Michelle dropped her purse and strutted over to where her husband sat with Jazzlyn—a little too close for her taste.

Damien Goodlove was the spitting image of his father. He was a younger version, and looked as if old man Goodlove had spit his son out of his own loins. But where his father sported a bald hairstyle, Damien's hair was in a stylish fade. He quickly jumped up the moment he noticed his wife approaching.

"You mind telling me what is going on here?"

"Ah, Michelle, ww-what are you doing here?" Damien stood and smiled at Michelle. His eyes shifted nervously around the bustling restaurant.

"The real question is what the hell are you doing with her?" Michelle took in everything about Jazzlyn. She was a petite woman. She wasn't cute, but had all the attributes that belonged to a pretty girl. Her cinnamon-colored skin was flawless, her thick, black hair ran down her back, and she had a fierce hourglass figure. The men in the church were already singing the praises of her "near-perfect ass," as they called it. But Jazzlyn's face was hideous.

"You remember Jazzlyn, um, from church, don't you?"

Michelle looked at the woman, then back at her husband. Jazzlyn had the nerve to smile, knowing her stacked teeth were already too large for her even bigger mouth.

"Hey, 'Chelle," she had the audacity to say.

Michelle looked down at her, rolled her eyes,

sucked her teeth, and then quickly turned her attention back to her husband.

"Again, I need to know why you are sitting up here, damn near hugged up with this jezebel," she hissed.

"Ah, it's Jazz-lyn," the silly girl corrected.

The driver carefully pulled the shiny, black Bentley up Blueridge's circular driveway and brought the car to a slow crawl near the tree-lined walkway that led to the massive oak double doors.

Blueridge was the name of the seven-acre estate Pastor Goodlove called home. His seventeen-room, custom built mansion had its own Olympic-sized swimming pool with a hot tub. There were basketball and tennis courts on the grounds, as well as a helipad for the times when Pastor Goodlove had to fly to a church in neighboring Port Arthur that bore his name. He founded that church as well.

When the car stopped, the driver opened his door and rushed to the passenger's side. But by then, Pastor Goodlove was already climbing out of the backseat.

"Will you need my services anymore this evening?" the driver asked humbly.

"I'll page you if I do. Thanks, Darren."

At fifty-eight, Pastor Goodlove's body was still as tight as most men half his age, thanks to his daily two-hour workout. He had muscles in his back, arms, legs, and although he no longer sported a six pack, he was still good to go. He walked up to the front door and let himself into the house. All was quiet from where he stood.

"Theola?" he called. When there was no answer, he looked around the foyer and up at the grand spiral staircase, then placed his keys on the nearby table. His voice echoed back at him as it bounced off the cathedral ceiling. It had been a long day. He'd left early after deciding not to visit Mt. Zion Baptist with the rest of his staff. He yawned, and then glanced at the stack of mail on the marble tabletop before strolling into his study.

The room was done in cherry oak with a massive floor to ceiling custom library. His home was really his sanctuary. He had a colossal HD flat screen TV that he used to watch the taped version of his weekly sermons. And the room was outfitted with a state of the art surround sound system. He even had a small refrigerator built into the cabinets on the opposite side of the bookshelves.

After he eased into his oversized Italian leather chair, he reached into a secret compartment in his desk and dug out the bottle of aged brandy. Pastor Goodlove spent many hours laboring over his beloved sermons in that very spot. This was also where he turned for much needed relief. He was a busy man, with mounting stress and endless needs, and sometimes a good stiff drink helped to clear his head.

Pastor Goodlove poured himself a glass of liquor, threw it back, and swallowed it in one gulp. He poured another one and started to sip. A serene sense of calm came over him until he heard her voice. Theola was always hounding him for sex at the most inappropriate times. Then when he did succumb to her, she would take forever to cum, frustrating him even more.

"Um, you looking for me, sweet daddy?" His wife, Theola, stood at his study doors wearing a pair of four-inch stilettos and a set of extra long pearls that dangled between her taut breasts.

"Hmm, you make a man want to come home to that kind of greeting all the time, Theola."

She sashayed over to him and squeezed her naked body between her husband and the huge oak desk. Theola hitched her behind onto the edge of the desk, placed one leg to his right, the other to his left and took his head between her hands.

"I know how to make my man *want* to come home, if you know what I mean." She guided his head downward and prepared herself for the sudden rush of pleasure she was expecting.

"Whoa, hold on a minute," Pastor Goodlove protested.

"What's wrong, daddy?" Theola cooed.

"I just wanna finish my drink. Nothing's wrong." He took one of her nipples between his thumb and forefinger, then squeezed. When he tried to raise the glass to his lips, Theola snatched it from his hands.

"Awww, baby," he huffed.

Theola held it beyond his reach, then quickly poured the liquor down the front of her body and watched as it splashed against her skin, running between her legs.

"Uh-ooh, um, I'm all wet, Daddy."

Pastor Goodlove looked at his wife and slowly shook his head. He had never had the kind of wild and kinky sex he experienced with Theola. After his wife of nearly forty years passed, he had several encounters, but none like those with Theola.

The way she locked her long legs around his head, neck, and hips, quickly convinced him that he should make her his wife. It seemed as if she could have sex for hours non-stop. At times, he had to hide from her just to get some rest, but when he couldn't get away, he quickly gave in.

Pastor Goodlove knew that marrying Theola would probably put a stop to some of the foolishness floating around the congregation. Sure he had fooled around in his early days with both women and men, but that was in his past. When he first got married, he decided being a heterosexual would best suit his promising future and he had been right. He knew some didn't think it right that he marry after losing his first wife, but he and only he knew what was best. He had hoped Theola would be just the distraction the church needed to stop asking questions about his private life, but it didn't take long for him to realize he had brought Theola into a firestorm of confusion. While he believed having a sweet young thing would help his image, he never envisioned the problems he would face with his very own congregation.

Each time he thought about the church elders, mostly those who had too much time on their hands, he told himself in time they'd see how happy Theola made him, and then they'd come around. However, they made it very clear that she would never get the respect they had willingly given to the late Mrs. Goodlove.

He licked his wife's nipples, ran his tongue down the path the liquor had flowed, and buried his face in her crotch.

"SSsssss, yesss, sweet daddy, right there," Theola cried.

"Ehh-hem. Am I interrupting something?"

Pastor Goodlove jumped up at the sound of his middle son Reginald's voice. Reginald looked nothing like the other Goodlove men. Where they were dark, he was light. Where they were tall and muscular, Reginald was thin and of average height.

"Damn, I was almost there, Daddy," Theola said, rolling her eyes.

Reginald stood at the door and waited for his father. He wore a look of disgust on his face as he watched Theola and his father. He didn't like anything about her; she didn't even try to cover herself when she saw him standing there. After a few minutes Reginald turned away, hoping his father would "adjust" himself.

"I need a minute," Pastor Goodlove finally said.

"More than a minute is more like it," Theola spat.

"Let me go take care of him. I'll be right back," he tried to reason.

"He can wait. You need to take care of me!" Theola didn't attempt to lower her voice. "I was almost there. You need to finish what you started here," she pouted.

When Pastor Goodlove got up to leave, she grabbed at his shirt.

"You always make some excuse to avoid finishing what you start, and I'm getting tired of it, Ethan. You need to do your husbandly duties. That damn church ain't the only thing that needs your attention around here, you know!"

Despite Theola's rants, Pastor Goodlove walked out of the room to talk with his son. When Reginald showed up, they usually discussed the state of the church's finances. They'd often think of ways to increase the Sweetwater PG's bottom line, and that was something Pastor Goodlove enjoyed more than anything else.

He remembered the days when he lived check to check, struggling to pay bills and keep creditors off his back. But he vowed to put those days in his past and he had. He came up with every single money making scheme under the sun until one stuck. He never imagined the wealth he had found standing in the pulpit.

CHAPTER 2

"**Y**ou know, you should really do something about her," Reginald said as he passed his father the financial documents.

Pastor Goodlove ignored his son as he scrutinized the numbers that just didn't add up. They walked out to the enclosed deck that ran along the backside of the enormous house where the pool and hot tub were housed.

"According to these numbers, we're down nearly 10 percent. I don't like this," Pastor Goodlove said, still looking at the figures.

"Well, um, I told you, you need to get a handle on Theola's spending. Just last month, in um, February, she spent something like twenty thousand. Yeah, that's right, twenty thousand dollars on clothes. I mean, I know you want her to have nice things, but that's crazy," Reginald insisted. Finally, his father looked up at him.

"Theola spent twenty thousand dollars on clothes in February?"

"Yeah, Pop, that's what I'm trying to tell you. But you act like you don't care what she does. I don't understand it, man. Hmm, the tail can't be that good," Reginald mumbled under his breath.

"You let me worry about Theola. You just work on these numbers. I don't like what I've been seeing in the past few months. By August we're headed to the Promised Land, and we can't go if the finances aren't straight," Pastor Goodlove threatened. "I told you, I don't want to take out any loans on this project. You got anything else?"

Reginald looked down at the ground. He used his hand to rub his near-bald head.

"Well, um, look, Gee, you should try to curb your spending a bit, too. I mean, um, at least until we finish the expansion. With gas prices climbing, we should think about you cutting down on using the helicopter. I mean, the pilot's fees alone are crazy. Then there are the plans for the new beach house down on the west end of Galveston Beach." Reginald looked away from his father.

"What are you saying, boy?" Pastor Goodlove stepped toward Reginald. "Look at me like a man. You saying I don't deserve these things, boy? Hmm, I don't think you realize just how hard I work. It takes talent to translate God's words into a message you young folk want to hear. Then there's my work with the ill and disenfranchised. The counseling, endless appearances, and let's not forget the weekly radio program. Hmm, I deserve what I got and then some. Let's not forget either; it's my talent that takes care of you and yours. But enough about me. At the beginning of the year, you talked about hiring grant writers to secure more money for the AIDS Center. I ain't heard another word about that." Pastor Goodlove stepped even closer to his son. He looked him straight in the eyes.

"I mean, what the hell am I paying you a whopping fifty thousand dollars a year for if you can't help increase the bottom line?"

Reginald scowled at his father's words.

"I'm still working on the grant writers. I'm meeting with two next week. They should be in place by the end of March."

Pastor Goodlove started fumbling with his clothes as Reginald went on about plans for the next two months. The pastor pulled his phone from his pocket and dialed his driver.

"I need you here in ten minutes," he said, before flipping the razor thin phone shut. "Is there anything else, Reginald?"

"No, I guess that's it. I, um, I'm going to Victoria Tuesday to meet with the developer. Can I take the helicopter?"

"Didn't you just tell me about logging time in that thing? Now you want to hop in it? Drive," Pastor Goodlove snapped.

"OK," Reginald said. Pastor Goodlove looked at his diamond encrusted Rolex watch.

"Tell Theola I had to go away on business for a couple of days." He left out of the back door to meet his driver.

Damien Goodlove explained to his wife that he merely ran into Jazzlyn outside the restaurant. He assured Michelle that things were not as they appeared when she walked in on them. He was only trying to comfort her, as he was often called to do since he was a deacon at Sweetwater PG.

Damien explained that Jazzlyn was having a hard

time with the women and men at the church. It seemed that her reputation was making it difficult for her to make female friends, and the men wouldn't leave her alone.

But the minute he was able to coax his wife back to her own table, he convinced Jazzlyn to leave the restaurant and promised he'd catch up with her later. Damien had been working on the sweet little Jazzlyn for weeks, and there was no way he was giving up just because he forgot where his wife and her gossiping friends liked to brunch after church.

Hours after that near mishap, he was about to reap the benefits of his weeks of wooing Jazzlyn. They were holed up inside a room at the Motel Six off Interstate 45, on the outskirts of Houston.

"I thought we were gonna get a nicer room, Dee," Jazzlyn said.

"Lemme see what you got on," Damien insisted. He felt like he had spent enough time and money on Jazzlyn, and he was ready to get some kind of return on his investment. He and Jazzlyn had been sneaking around for nearly two weeks.

Each time he tried to take things to the next level, she came up with some lame excuse about why they couldn't do it. He wasn't about to give her any room for excuses this time.

Jazzlyn peered around the corner from the bathroom.

"You ready for me?" she teased.

Damien was tired of the games. He wanted her in a bad way, and he had the most painful hard-on to prove it. He sat waiting on the edge of the bed.

When Jazzlyn walked out of the room, she was a

heavenly sight. She wore a little gold lace number that barely covered her large breasts. Her body was even better than the other deacons had described. Damien could hardly believe his good fortune. He had something for Jazzlyn, and he couldn't wait to give all of it to her.

"I really hope this brings us closer," she said.

"Um, yeah, why don't you turn around real quick?" He rubbed his crotch and nearly started drooling when he caught a glimpse of her plump behind and the little tiny gold string that seemed lost between her juicy cheeks. She looked sluttish in the outfit, and he liked it.

"Come here, girl," he said.

"Wait, I wanna talk first, Damien. Remember when I was telling you about my experience over at Wilshire Baptist? I guess I'm just, um, I don't know, a bit afraid. See, I don't want to make the same mistake again. I'm ready for something real—a husband. Um, you know, a man of the cloth. And I know, well, I know you're not in charge at Sweetwater, but everybody knows you're in line for . . . um, Damien, I can't concentrate when you do that," Jazzlyn said.

"You don't like it?" he whispered.

"No. I mean, it's not that, it's just we got all the time in the world to get to that. I just want to set some ground rules before we, well, you know . . ."

Damien took his thick chocolate finger and forcefully inserted it into Jazzlyn's moist opening.

"Sssssss," she playfully slapped his shoulder. "Will you stop it? I'm, I'm trying to tell you something." She giggled.

Instead of stopping, Damien pulled the crotch of

the teddy to one side and rammed three more fingers into Jazzlyn. He stared deeply into her eyes as his fingers explored her.

"We didn't come here to talk, Jazz."

"Yeah, but you could at least try to spend some time with me." She released a heavy breath.

Damien twisted his fingers deep inside her flesh and marveled at the way the feeling made her eyes roll up into the back of her head. She snickered.

"You like that?" he asked, eyeing her closely. She grabbed at his hand.

"Wait, boo, I'm tryin' ta, ooohhh, I'm um . . ." She started gyrating her hips against his hand. "Damn, Dee, there you go . . . you hittin' my spot already."

"Yeah, girl, I'm about to be way up in you in a minute. You like that, huh?"

Jazzlyn bit down on her bottom lip. She struggled to stop herself from screaming. She moved her hips and squeezed her thighs together.

Damien, even more excited than before, used his free hand to pinch her nipples. He gently slapped her left breast, watched it bounce out of the teddy, and then slopped it with his moist tongue. He caught her nipple and held it tightly between his teeth.

"Sssss . . . I need you to um, to www-wait." Jazzlyn fought herself. "We gotta talk about what this is gonna mean. Oooh wee, you know, when we're through."

Tired of hearing her talk, Damien took her hand and guided it to his enormous member. At first touch, she pulled her hand away as if she was touching sheer fire. But he easily steered it back.

"Ooooh, it's soooooo—" Jazzlyn struggled to catch her breath as Damien's fingers moved in and out of her quickly.

Satisfied that she might be ready for what he had to offer, he removed his fingers, sniffed them, and then suckled each one like he was savoring candy. As he did this, Jazzlyn's eyes locked on his.

"Pull that chair over here," he demanded.

Jazzlyn did exactly what he asked. When the chair was right where Damien wanted it, he removed the last of his clothes and placed the chair a few inches from the bed. He took Jazzlyn by the hand.

"You trust me?" he asked.

She nodded and allowed him to guide her closer to the chair.

"OK, look at this. I'm gonna sit on the chair and lean back." Damien tilted the chair until it leaned comfortably on the mattress. "Here, push on it; you see how sturdy it is on this mattress. I'm not gonna let you get hurt, OK?"

"Why we gotta have it leaning like that?" she asked.

"'Cause that's gonna help me get way up in you, real deep. That's how you like it, right? I just wanted you to see that the chair is sturdy against the mattress."

"Um, ah, OK," Jazzlyn said.

Damien placed the chair back to its upright position and pulled his boxers to his ankles. Jazzlyn's eyes nearly bulged from their sockets.

"You OK?" he asked, beaming with pride.

"Um . . ." Her eyes stayed glued to his member.

Damien stroked himself, hoping she wasn't about to try to back out now that she had gotten him all worked up.

"Here, why don't you touch it? I swear it won't bite," he assured.

"I'm not worrying about being bitten," she said.

As soon as Damien's hands left hers, Jazzlyn pulled her hand away from his crotch.

"You're not scared, are you?" he asked gently.

"Nah, it's just, um. I ain't never seen one like that. I mean, how it get so big and thick?"

"Good genes, baby. Goodlove genes to be exact. Don't worry, you'll enjoy it," he promised. Before she could say another word in protest, Damien pulled out a tube of KY Jelly. "If you like, we could use some of this, but I think you can handle it."

Jazzlyn looked back and forth between Damien, his large member, and the jelly he held in his hand. She didn't say a word.

"C'mon, girl. I promise it'll only hurt for a minute, then it'll get good for you." Noticing the time, Damien sat on the chair and extended his hands toward Jazzlyn.

She stepped toward him and started to remove the teddy that was now completely soaked with her wetness. The smell of raw sex lingered in the air. The room was hot and muggy. Damien pulled out the black and gold condom wrapper. Once it was on as best as he could fit it, she carefully swung one leg over the left side of the chair.

"You ready?" he asked. Jazzlyn took a deep breath, then exhaled.

"Here, play with my titties. That'll help."

"Look, don't worry about none of that. I'm gonna take care of everything. I'll help you get on, then once you all comfy, I'll handle everything else. I just want you to hang on and enjoy yourself, cool?"

"Um, OK."

At first, the head of Damien's member sat at her

opening. She wiggled her hips and worked more of him into her slowly.

But after a few minutes, Damien started getting impatient. He was ready to beat up on her walls. When she was halfway on his member, he took her by the hips and shoved himself as far as he could go up into her.

She released a strained yelp, but it didn't take long for her to start moving her hips. After a while, her moans went from belly wrenching gasps to sheer squeals of pleasure, which was music to Damien's ears.

Barry Goodlove read the letter for the seventh time. The words had long etched themselves onto his brain, but still, he couldn't bring himself to believe what he was reading.

He had no idea how things had gone so terribly wrong. Oh how he wished he could be more like his whoring brother Damien. Married for eight years now, Damien changed women like he changed shoes, and Michelle seemed just as dumb as they come.

But that just wasn't Barry's style. When his mother was alive, he knew he had been her favorite. They used to talk about his future, one that involved a good Christian woman, a true helpmate. He would be the one to make both his blood and church families proud.

Now he sat wondering just how he had strayed so far off the path, and worse, he just didn't see any way for him to find his way back into God's good graces.

It all started when he was asked to help out with the church's youth ministry. Barry had no desire to follow in his father's footsteps, but he was a God-fearing man who was very religious. His walk with God had been a good one, and although he'd slip up from time to time, sipping a little drink here and there, he was a born again virgin and was doing real good until Sissy Briggs started coming to Sweetwater. She had a part time job at a non profit organization that did work with the church, and soon she was volunteering in the church's youth program.

When he first laid eyes on her olive-colored skin, he felt an instant burning sensation deep in his loins. Her dreamy eyes, framed by the thickest set of lashes, were so brown he thought they were black. He could hardly resist staring into them for endless hours.

That had been three months ago, and since then things had gone downhill faster than he ever thought possible.

What would the ladies or mothers of the church say? Moreover, what would his father say? How could he ever repair his tarnished image?

Barry refolded the letter and tucked it back into his wallet the moment he heard the shower cut off. He had been waiting for Amy for nearly an hour.

He and Amy were supposed to get married as soon as they both completed the master's program at the University of Houston next fall. They were planning a winter wedding. Well, it was more like she and her family had planned everything. Amy came from a strict, Christian home. Her parents had raised her to put God first in everything, especially when picking a potential mate.

Amy was why the church was so proud of Barry. He was in his junior year of college, and was planning to marry into the second largest black church family in Houston. Amy's father, the Bishop Howard Blackwell, ran Houston's Premier Biblical Institute.

Their engagement had even made the *Houston Chronicle*'s society pages. It was Barry's mother who told him that a couple lines without a picture cost more than twenty-five hundred dollars. His and Amy's spread was a whole half page. Yes, he had made Sweetwater PG proud, but that was before Sissy Briggs. Until he came up with a plan, Barry knew he had to stay on Sissy's good side at all costs. The last thing he wanted for her to do was tip her hand. According to the letter, she was ready and prepared to face their Sweetwater family with the truth about their good boy, Barry. And that was a truth that would surely set off a scandal that would bring both families a considerable amount of embarrassment. He couldn't bear the thought of it.

He absolutely had to find a way out of this mess, because the alternative just seemed too grim.

CHAPTER 3

The band and choir started up again at full throttle and Pastor Goodlove broke into his famous strut, bringing to close yet another heart-filled sermon.

"I saaaid, hello somebody." Pastor Goodlove had started shuffling from one end of the pulpit to the next.

"Baby, you can't deal with your issues until you recognize and admit you have an issue!" The pastor put his hand up to his ear and cupped it. "Is there anybody out there?" Parishioners jumped to their feet.

"I said, until you recognize you have an issue and own up to it, you can't deal with it. See, your way is not *the* way."

"Preach, Pastor, preach!" a voice yelled from the very back of the room.

"Your problem is all yours baby, until you pass it on to the Lord." The congregation was up on its feet, dancing, shuffling around, and rejoicing in the pastor's electrifying sermon.

Mama Sadie began wheezing in an attempt to

catch her breath. Before she could stumble, the rest of the holy rollers were by her side. The holy rollers were a group of church elders who made it their life's mission to decide and determine which behavior God might deem worthy. It was an unsolicited job they took very seriously at Sweetwater Powerhouse of God. Behind their backs, members dubbed them the holy rollers because although they were some of the biggest sinners themselves, they judged others as if they were designated to pass out blessings from God himself.

Rumor had it that at least two of them had a gambling problem. One ran a small-time brothel in her heyday, and some members of Sweetwater insisted that Mama Sadie religiously added something from a silver flask to her morning mug. Still, she and the holy rollers designated themselves judge, jury, and executioner of any sin they heard about, witnessed, or believed they could sidetrack in an attempt to protect Sweetwater PG's image.

Pastor Goodlove paused at the pulpit. His massive back was erect, his almond-shaped eyes were focused, and his handsome face was drenched in sweat. As he scanned his congregation, his heartbeat returned to its normal rate. He lived for this very moment each and every Sunday. Soon his voice began to fade in and out as he walked back and forth and side to side. He started to sing slowly.

"I feel him!"

Just then, the screams from the congregation began and pandemonium soon followed as the members fell into the spirit of God. Every foot was stomping and many people started shouting, "Yes, Lord!" and "Yes, sir!"

The screams had grown so loud and thunderous that they threatened to drown out the animated reverend. He closed his sermon with a recommendation to get right with God, which was followed by a closing hymn from the choir.

As the pastor looked out at his parishioners, he marveled at just how far he had come. The former small-time crook and twice-convicted felon was now at the helm of one of Houston's largest and most prestigious churches, and each week their membership classes seemed to swell. Sweetwater even had a waiting list for its membership classes!

Satisfied that his performance had the effect he intended, Pastor Goodlove walked away from his platform as an assistant pastor stepped up to close out service for the morning.

This gave Pastor Goodlove the opportunity to retire to his private chambers for a shower and a change of clothes. By the time he finished and reappeared in crisp, fresh clothes, the last offering would be in its final stage and he'd prepare to bid the parishioners goodbye.

As the members began to pour out of the church, Michelle waited to see what her husband's plans were for the rest of the day. She'd deliberately held off on plans with her girls to make sure Damien didn't feel the need to take any wayward ladies out for brunch.

Michelle couldn't read the look she saw across her husband's face as he approached.

"You OK, hon?" She smiled as two young ladies scurried past her, giggling.

"I'm just tired and Pops wants me to go out to Blueridge this evening," Damien huffed.

Struggling to hide her disappointment, Michelle smiled as another group passed and hurried out of the door.

"Why do you have to go out there? I mean, you do have a family. It's been so long since we've been together after church." Michelle stopped complaining as more people passed. Finally, she grabbed her husband by the arm.

"Wha-what are you doing? Where are we going?" he asked.

"I'm gonna go talk to the G-man myself. I'm sure if I explain to him that we need some family time, he'll opt to go with Reginald or even Barry instead. This is ridiculous!" she snapped.

"Wait a minute, babe. Hold up a sec. I don't think that's a good idea. You know how the old man can be sometimes. The last thing I want is for him to think I ain't running my own house. You and the girls go eat, and I'll catch up with you later. I promise."

"That ain't good enough, Damien." Michelle was furious. She had a gut feeling that her husband was lying and up to his old tricks again, but in hopes of avoiding a very public argument, she decided to let his lame story fly.

"So, when do you think you'll be home?" she asked. Michelle didn't even try to mask the impatient look on her face. As Damien spoke, she kept thinking about how Jazzlyn had snuck out of church just when the choir had started closing out service. Oh, how she prayed he wasn't sneaking off to be with that tramp.

The rumors had already started flying around the church, but she'd been praying that they were only rumors this time.

". . . so if I'm lucky, I'll get in sometime before ten," he was saying.

"Why don't I bring the kids and we can go over there with you?" she asked out of desperation.

"Nah, the sooner I get to Blueridge, the sooner I get back. Besides, I don't want the kids there distracting the old man. Ain't no telling what time we'll get home if that happens."

Before Michelle could protest anymore, Damien reached over and pecked her cheek.

"I'll be sure and call if I'm gonna be later." He started toward the door. "Oh, don't wait up," he said.

Michelle swallowed back tears as two of the church elders passed.

"You OK, baby?" Ms. Elaine asked.

She nodded, and then rushed off to the youth section to find the girls. Michelle was tired of Damien and his constant running around. It was like he and the other deacons at Sweetwater PG competed to see who could tap the new women the fastest. And it seemed as though new women were flowing into Sweetwater quicker than she could count.

After that encounter with her husband, she wasn't even in the mood for brunch. She figured she'd grab her daughters and sneak out the side door. Later, she'd explain to Tammy and Kim why she didn't show up. That's if she was even in the mood to do any explaining. If she wasn't, oh well, too bad.

Although they were her friends, she knew for a fact that when her husband started running around again, Kim and Tammy were sure to be right in the middle of the flying rumors.

Behind the wheel of her SUV, Michelle thought about trying to figure out just where her husband had really gone.

She didn't buy that line about Blueridge for a minute. Instead of driving toward their house in North Houston, she decided to take the girls to Chuck E. Cheese. After they finished there, she'd make a decision about whether she should show up at her father-in-law's house to catch her husband in yet another one of his elaborate lies.

Pastor Goodlove regretted his decision to personally see his parishioners off the moment his wife sashayed up to him. She could barely move her legs in the pencil skirt that looked like it had been painted on.

As she approached, he noticed the dress she was wearing was more suited for an after-hour juke joint than a house of worship. The pastor swallowed the bad taste forming in his mouth. He had told Theola a dozen times to tone it down a bit, but still she continued to push it.

"Hey, daddy," she cooed.

"Theola! Not now," he snapped.

"Well, when then? I mean, I haven't seen you in a few days now. C'mon, let's go to the back so we can talk," she said.

Pastor Goodlove kept his eyes on other church members as they passed and threw Theola looks of disdain mixed with disgust.

"Theola, why must you continue to dress like a

street walker? You have an image to uphold as first lady of Sweetwater." He smiled at one of his assistant pastors.

"Oh come on . . . not you too. Don't tell me they got to you. Those holy rollers won't quit until I'm outta here. You think I don't know their plans, especially that Mama Sadie, with her mean ole self," Theola spat.

Pastor Goodlove grabbed her by the arm. They quickly walked toward the back of the church and slipped into his chambers.

"Theola, you know this is a stressful time for Sweetwater. I need your support. Showing up looking like some two-bit ho ain't helping."

"Well, I remember a time when you used to lust after this two-bit ho." Theola used her hands to pull the dress down. Each time she moved, it rode up her thighs. Pastor Goodlove shook his head.

"Theola, I'm not calling you a ho, I'm just saying, I could use some cooperation on your part, that's all."

"You wanna talk about cooperation? Well, what about that damn Sadie and her holier than thou pack? I've asked you to talk to them. They continue to disrespect me and you do nothing. Do you know those old hags had the nerve to pull me aside and try to tell me what kind of clothes I should be wearing up in here?" She hopped up onto the desk and crossed her legs. "That's why I hand-selected this number, just for them. You should've seen the way they stared at me when I strolled in today." She chuckled.

"And black, Theola?" He shook his head and resolved that there was no point in trying to reason with her. Theola was going to be Theola no matter what he said, and he knew it, there was just no way to change her into someone or something she was not.

"I'll take care of Sadie and the other elders," he said.

"That's not good enough for me, Ethan. I want to be there when you talk to them. I want you to tell them that they need to respect me, and if they don't, you should tell them to find another church home. I'm sick of being treated like some little insignificant nobody around here." Theola spread her legs and leaned forward.

Pastor Goodlove looked between them, then up at her. He closed his eyes.

"Theola! Please don't tell me you've been switching around here with no panties on!" He sighed. "What am I gonna do with you?"

She hopped off the desk and walked over to the sofa.

"I have a few ideas." She smiled.

"Look, this isn't the time. Besides, I need to talk to you about your shopping. You spent twenty thousand dollars on clothes in one month's time? That's insane," he hissed.

"I don't know what you're talking about, daddy. I haven't been shopping in months, and the last time I went, I damn—" Theola put her fingers to her lips. "Ooops, I mean, I haven't spent that kind of money since I went to the Bahamas, and you knew all about that trip."

Pastor Goodlove made a mental note to double check the numbers Reginald had turned in.

CHAPTER 4

Pastor Goodlove squeezed his eyes shut. He struggled to relish the moment. Powerful hands were doing wonders on his sore muscles. He enjoyed therapeutic massages nearly as much as he enjoyed great sex. He had a standing appointment every Wednesday afternoon. The massages were great, but rough, raw, and rugged sex was his absolute favorite.

"Why don't you use more of that stuff? You know, the stuff that burns when you rub it in," he suggested.

The masseuse used both hands to add pressure to the pastor's shoulder blades. It was a move the pastor really enjoyed. Then the masseuse applied the sports rub that was usually reserved for the athletic clients.

As the pastor began to relax, the sensations started to stir something different deep within him. He tried to fight the feeling, but once he felt the ice-cold liquid that instantly warmed at his masseuse's touch, Pastor Goodlove was immediately turned on.

"That feels super," he cooed.

Pastor Goodlove wasn't sure what he should do.

These things were always very tricky. He had to be very careful about his approach. This was only the third time he had used this masseuse, so he didn't want any misunderstandings.

When the pastor felt the strong hands moving toward his lower back, his balls started to tingle. When those hands traveled down to his behind, he decided he didn't have anything to lose.

"You like that?" the masseuse asked softly.

Pastor Goodlove didn't respond. He was too busy trying to regulate his breathing. It had been so long since he had experienced such a sensational sexual rush without penetration. The masseuse's strokes became stronger and more intense.

"This is just what the doctor ordered. You know exactly what I like. You understand I'm prepared to reward you generously for this, right?"

The masseuse chuckled and continued to carefully knead the knots in the pastor's thighs. The soft jazz that played through hidden speakers helped Pastor Goodlove relax even more. At times thoughts floated through his mind, but he tried to fight them off.

When the masseuse's hands traveled up from his ankles, to his thighs, lingered at his back side, then slid up to his shoulders, Pastor Goodlove thought he would bust a nut right there on the table. He lifted his head ever so slightly.

"Hey, why don't I turn over so we can work on the front a bit?"

Pastor Goodlove waited for the masseuse to step back. He balanced himself on the table, making sure the sheet used for cover slid to the floor.

He watched carefully as the masseuse's eyes

locked on his stiff erection. They smiled at each other. Pastor Goodlove made his member do a little dance that brought a sinister chuckle from the masseuse.

"I like that," the masseuse said.

"I was hoping you would," the Pastor confirmed. After that exchange, the pastor didn't waste any time moving in for the sinful—but sweet—kill.

Damien watched closely as Jazzlyn walked around to the front of the sofa. He had upgraded their meeting place to the Homewood Suites. He noticed right away that she put a little extra twist in her sashay, and he liked it.

"So, lemme see, what if I promised to suck you off to sleep, then awake again?" Jazzlyn sat very close to Damien. Using her index finger, she touched her moistened lips. "Um, I don't know." She stuck her chest outward. "Hmm, like this?" Jazzlyn slowly and deliberately sucked her finger, then used it to trace a wet path through her overflowing bosom. Damien's eyes nearly popped out of their sockets.

"You know I'm married, Jazz. I got a wife and kids. Michelle's gonna . . . um, I just can't stay all night."

"Yeah, I know, but can't I do anything to convince you otherwise?" She pouted her glossy red lips. He shook his head.

"I can't let my kids down like that. 'Sides, I don't want Michelle tripping."

"Yeah, I understand. But, um, I was hoping I could do something to change your mind. We could always say something real important came up." She flicked her hair over her shoulder.

Damien watched as Jazzlyn's hands traveled from her breasts to her mid section, then down to her legs. When she saw his gaze stop at her crotch, she used both hands to dramatically spread her legs.

"I'm willing to do whatever it takes to get what I want."

Damien swallowed.

"Now, you know I'm good at keeping secrets, but I'm kind of tired of lurking behind the scenes. I think you should spend the night a few times. I guess you can say I'm willing to work to help change your mind. You know, like the kitty kat." Jazzlyn smiled.

"The kitty kat?" Damien asked, all but drooling as he spoke.

"Never mind that. So how long can you stay out tonight?"

"I just can't stay all night, Jazz. That's all I'm saying." Jazzlyn sighed. She looked around the living room again.

"Well," she said as she slipped off her shoes, "I guess we might as well get comfy. 'Cause I'm prepared to do whatever it takes to get my man to spend the night, the whole night with me."

"Well, I'm telling you now, Jazz, it ain't gonna happen." Damien's eyes were glued to her shapely legs. Jazzlyn got up from the sofa and walked toward the bedroom.

"Hey, where are you going?" He jumped up and followed her. "I can't guarantee your safety if you decide to go back there," he mumbled.

By the time he walked all the way into the bedroom, Jazzlyn was sprawled across the king-sized bed. She lifted her head slightly and looked at Damien, who stood at the door.

"Emmm." She patted the spot next to her. "Why don't you join me?"

Damien didn't leave his perch. He watched as Jazzlyn spread her legs. His heart rate increased and he started feeling warm.

"OK, suit yourself. Stay there, but I'm not responsible for what happens after you see what you may see from there." She rolled over and elevated her rear as she pushed herself up on her knees.

"Wh . . ." Damien swallowed. "Why are you playing, being a tease?" He could barely steady his voice.

"Why don't you come in here and spank me," Jazzlyn cooed.

Damien wanted to fuck her until she cried for him to stop. He knew she wanted him to stay, but he made it very clear that he was not leaving his family. Now that they'd been sneaking around, she was making all kinds of demands. If her pussy wasn't so tight and sweet, he would consider leaving her alone all together. But the truth was, he was hooked. Every time he tried to stop, it was like Jazzlyn's sweet little twat kept calling him right back.

"I don't want any confusion here, Jazzlyn. You knew the rules when we started, so why are you tripping now?" Damien eased a little closer to the bed. Jazzlyn turned over, so she could see him.

"It's like this. We are sooo good together, but when you get up and leave me in the wee hours of the morning, it makes me feel cheap. You enjoy what we do, and I know you can't get it this good at home, so why don't we just come clean with wifey once and for all?"

Damien considered walking out at that very moment. He knew that despite what he said, continuing to fuck Jazzlyn could only lead to trouble. But when he looked up and saw the perfectly–shaped pubic hair triangle between her thighs, he was rendered defenseless. Soon, the only head with any independent thought was the one between his very own legs.

Sissy left the beauty salon and rushed to her next appointment. She wasn't about to leave anything to chance. She had planned the evening down to the second. When she arrived at the address in the Galleria area, she called the jeweler to let him know she was turning into his parking lot. She turned her keys over to the valet and watched as the security guard unlocked the door.

"Ms. Briggs?"

"Yes," she confirmed.

"What time is your appointment?" an attendant asked.

"Two fifteen. Is he ready?"

"He's running a little behind. But if you'll wait a few minutes, he's just wrapping up. Would you care for a glass of wine or bottled water?"

"Wine sounds great. Red?"

"Of course."

Just as the attendant arrived with the wine, Mr. Holstein came out from behind thick black curtains to greet Sissy.

"Ms. Briggs. How are you today?"

She stood, accepted her wine, and followed the little balding man behind the curtains.

"I'm good. Thanks for asking."

"Your order is in, and I think you'll be pleasantly surprised with the design."

"Great. I'm in a hurry, so let's see what you have for me."

"Of course." The man sat at a stool and opened a drawer to his left. He pulled out a small velvet bag and shook out a small box.

Sissy watched his every move.

He opened the small burgundy box and flipped it open. Once he examined its contents, he extended the box toward Sissy. She gasped and placed a hand on her chest.

"Oh my." The man smiled.

"I thought you'd be pleased."

"This is far better than I envisioned," she confessed. He gave her his eyepiece.

"Its clarity is remarkable," he said,

Sissy took a closer look at the three-carat stone. It was embedded in the middle of smaller baguettes and had a shine that forced her to blink.

"This is absolutely beautiful."

"I knew you'd like it. Satisfied?" he asked.

Sissy removed the platinum engagement ring from the box. She held it up for another inspection before slipping it onto her ring finger.

"Oh, this is simply breathtaking. It looks so wonderful."

"Do you think it will be to your friend's liking?"

"Oh, of course. You did a terrific job!" She took the ring off her finger and placed it back in the box. The man gave her the little velvet bag. "Now, what's the remaining balance?" she asked.

"Twenty-five sixty and seventy-four cents." Sissy removed her checkbook from her purse.

"OK, that's two thousand five hundred sixty dollars and seventy-four cents." She signed her name and gave the check to the old man.

"If you'll excuse me, allow me to gift wrap that for you?" he said, before leaving Sissy alone in the small room.

When he returned, the bag was in a fancier bag that was tied with a velvet bow. The man gave her both the bag and another business card.

"Please come see us again."

"Most definitely."

Sissy climbed into her car and drove to Nordstrom's at the Galleria. There she walked to the specialty shop where her dress was waiting for her to pick up.

"OK, got the ring, dress, now it's time to head to the house," she mumbled as she made her way back to the parking lot.

Hours later, she was on her way to Barry's condo. Things had been so much better now that he understood how serious she was about their future together. And Sissy was determined to hang on to the good times.

She had made reservations for them at Sullivan's, and she didn't want to be late. They'd enjoy a wonderful steak and lobster dinner, then move to the back for dancing. If everything worked out like she'd planned, she would never have to worry about problems with Amy again.

She knew and understood it wouldn't be easy for Barry to forget about Amy, but Sissy knew her patience and persistence would eventually pay off. At times he still talked about Amy while they were together. She figured that might threaten most women, but Sissy didn't mind. Actually, she encouraged Barry to share his feelings. She figured it was the best way for her to eventually snuff Amy out for good.

"Dinner was great. Actually, the entire evening was just what I needed," Barry was saying as he navigated his way back to his condo. "And, where'd you learn to dance like that?" he teased. Sissy was thrilled.

"Oh, I've always been able to hold my own."

"I'll second that. Shoot, you were trying to wear me out." She pouted.

"Well, I hope you're not too tired. The grand finale is still to come."

"I don't know if I can handle much more." Barry carefully guided his car into his parking lot.

"I promise I'll take it easy on you for the rest of the night." She smiled wickedly. Sissy sat and waited for Barry to come around and open her car door.

Inside his place, she lit candles and turned on soft music while he showered. By the time he got out of the shower, she had changed into the outfit she ordered from a Frederick's of Hollywood catalog.

The look on Barry's face told her he was more than a little bit surprised.

When he took a seat on the couch, she had two glasses of wine waiting. He reached for one, but she tapped his hand.

"Not yet. You're jumping the gun."

"Oh?" He snatched his hand back. "Just let me know."

Sissy got up and started rubbing his bare shoulders. She applied a dab of vanilla oil and started rubbing more intensely.

"That feels so good," he whispered.

"I'm glad you enjoyed yourself tonight."

"Thank you so much, Sissy. You're really helping me through a hard time. With school and everything going on at Sweetwater, it's good to have someone to talk to."

"Ssshh." She moved to face him and put a finger to her pursed lips. "Let's not talk about church. Not tonight," she whispered. Sissy started showering his neck and chest with soft, wet kisses.

"You mean so much to me," she said, falling to her knees in front of him. "I only want to make you happy. Everything I do, I think of you and us." She looked up. "You know that, don't you?"

He nodded. Sissy took his face into the palms of her hands.

"I know you're not exactly where I am just yet, but if I'm nothing else, Barry, you know I'm patient. I don't mind giving you time to get over Amy, because I know this is where you belong, where we belong, together. I know how to make you happy."

Barry blinked quickly.

"I can't begin to explain how much I love you. How I've loved you. We're good together and we make a wonderful team. I know you can learn to love me, and I'm willing to wait."

Barry frowned a bit, but he didn't interrupt. Sissy could tell he was probably wondering just where this was going.

Sissy backed up. Still on her knees, she reached behind her back and produced the small box. She gazed into Barry's eyes longingly.

"I want you to know that no matter what happens here tonight, I will always love you as I always have."

"Hey, what's going on?" he asked, suddenly finding his voice.

"Ssshhh, let me finish." Sissy cleared her throat. She took a deep breath, closed her eyes, exhaled, and then looked at Barry. "OK, as I was saying, I've known since the day I first laid eyes on you at Sweetwater's youth social that you were the man for me. Everything I've done since then has been to get us here. I've worked hard for you. I'm prepared to endure the stares and whispers when we're around our church family. I know that there are so many people who believe you and Amy should be together, but I know what I want." Sissy swallowed hard. She struggled to steady her voice. "Well, that's why, um, I want to know if you'll give me the honor of being your wife?" She waited for the words to register.

At first, her heart sank a bit when frown lines appeared on Barry's forehead. He looked perplexed.

"Ah, what?" he asked as she flipped open the small box. "I picked this up today." Barry looked at the ring, then back at her. He shook his head slightly.

"What do you mean, you picked this up today? Is that what I think it is, an engagement ring?" he asked, baffled.

"Wait, Barry. Don't answer yet. I want you to think about it. But I just wanted you to know how serious I am about this, about us, about our future."

"But you bought an engagement ring? Like, for yourself?"

"Um, I know you and Amy are sort of engaged, but I was hoping you'd well, um. You're gonna call it off with her anyway, right?" Barry blinked a few times.

"So you went out and bought your own engagement ring?"

She nodded, but remained silent. Sissy wanted to

know what he was thinking and what he was feeling, but he didn't say anything for a few minutes. Her heart started racing. This wasn't how it was supposed to go. She had planned this evening right down to the very moment she'd ask the question.

It's why the wine was standing by. He was supposed to be thrilled, surprised by her progressive attitude and her ambition for going after what she wanted.

Before he could say another word, Sissy pulled the ring out and slipped it onto her trembling finger.

"I only wanted to let you know how serious I am about us."

"So, not only do you propose, but you've already gone out and bought your own damn ring?" Barry shook his head. "Who goes out and buys their own damn ring? You didn't feel just a little bit funny doing that? I mean, you bought an engagement ring for yourself!" he snapped.

Sissy let him finish his rampage. She watched as his nostrils flared, his forehead wrinkled, and his brows shot up. When she was certain he had gotten it all out, she spoke calmly.

"Barry, I don't know how else to prove my love for you." Deep down inside she knew her way was best. If left alone, Barry could go either way the wind blew. "You don't have to answer now, but would you at least give it some thought, just consider it? We'd make one helluva team. Besides, remember what I said in the letter," she mumbled.

It was as if she hadn't heard a word he said. Barry was speechless. He watched on as Sissy admired her new engagement ring. His eyes narrowed when she mentioned the letter. He couldn't believe she could blackmail him so easily, and then expect him to want to be with her.

"So when are we gonna announce our good news to our church family?" Sissy asked with a straight face.

Barry looked mortified.

CHAPTER 5

"**A**nd I say, uh, I say, where you came from don't look nothing like where you're going." Pastor Goodlove pranced from one end of the pulpit to the other. With his arms waving and sweat dripping from his forehead he screamed. "Hello, somebody!"

"Amen, Pastor!" the voices screamed. Pastor Goodlove shuffled his feet.

"I said, hello somebody?"

Rows of people stood, some swaying to silent music, others stomping their feet. Most were shedding tears.

"Hallelujah! Pastor, Hallelujah!" Pastor Goodlove looked toward the sea of faces.

"Know that when God is the captain of your ship, your future looks a whole lot brighter than your past!"

Before the assistant pastor could ask God to bestow traveling grace onto his brothers and sisters,

Theola was up on her stilettos and twisting her red leather mini-skirted hips toward the back of the church. The elders who sat in the front pew immediately began to whisper back and forth.

"Ole heathen," someone said loud enough for most to hear.

"She didn't even have her finger up," someone else mumbled.

Theola was fired up because she hadn't seen or heard from her husband in nearly a week. She knew he'd show up for service, and she was right.

"Ethan Ezeekel Goodlove the third!" Theola snapped as she barged into Pastor Goodlove's chambers. "Do you realize I have not seen you in seven entire days? What kind of marriage is this?"

"I don't have time, Theola. I'm due in Beaumont in less than an hour. The chopper is already on the helipad. We'll talk about this later."

"We will talk about this now. I did not get married to be sitting home all by myself!"

When Pastor Goodlove emerged from his private bathroom, he was dressed in a navy tailored suit. He held up a finger to hush Theola.

"If I'm lucky, I'll be home by sundown. Now, I don't have time for this. I need to run. We'll talk later.

Before she could protest anymore, Pastor Goodlove was out his side door and rushing to the waiting helicopter.

"So what are you gonna do about this bitch? Y'all see what that skank wore to church today? I couldn't believe it. She looked like she strolled right out of the club and into the sanctuary," Tammy hissed. Kim looked at Michelle with narrowing eyes.

"We're your girls, so you know we're not gonna be sitting around talking about you, but word is she and your man have been getting buck wild for months now! What are you gonna do? I say, we whoop her ass!"

Michelle couldn't believe what she was hearing. It's not that she didn't think her husband was capable of such things—deep down inside she knew he cheated. But in the history of their marriage, she couldn't remember a time when he cheated with the same skank repeatedly.

She saw the fire in her friends' eyes, but didn't know how to respond. They were standing at the back of the church. Most of the people were still working their way toward the doors. Kim and Tammy wanted Michelle to say she'd do something to Jazzlyn, but the truth was that she was sick and tired of going through this with her husband. It seemed every few months it was someone new.

Just as Michelle was about to respond, Mama Sadie and two of the holy rollers made their way toward the back. Kim and Tammy moved over, thinking the women were trying to pass. Instead, they stopped in front of Michelle.

Mama Sadie wore a bright purple, ankle length skirt suit. It was made of polyester with decorative stones and faux fur lining the cuffs and neckline. She had a wide-brimmed hat, made out of the same material, with giant peacock-like feathers sticking out of the top. The other woman, Geraldine Brown, wore a simple pale-green skirt suit with a small pillbox hat. Tight, black curls spilled out of the hat and cascaded down her back.

"We needs to speak with you," Mama Sadie said directly to Michelle. She then looked at Tammy and Kim as if to wonder why they were still there.

"Well, Mama Sadie, we were just about to go to brunch. Would you and Ms. Geraldine like to come?" Michelle asked. Kim tossed Tammy a bewildered look.

"We've got plans of our own chile, but thanks. I really wanted to have a discreet word with you. It won't hold you up too long," Mama Sadie assured her.

"Why don't we just meet you at the restaurant?" Tammy offered.

Before Michelle could agree, Mama Sadie was already ushering her off to the Women's Auxiliary room. Ms. Geraldine shut the door behind them.

"As the moral watchdogs for Sweetwater PG," Mama Sadie started as Michelle struggled to keep a straight face. "We feel it our duty to strongly suggest that you and your husband seek counseling. Now we realize that because of your father-in-law's position, that might be somewhat uncomfortable. So we have taken it upon ourselves to speak with Second Assistant Pastor McCain. He heads up the marriage ministry. And well, we've already alerted him to the sensitive nature of the situation, and he's agreed to meet with you and Damien."

Michelle felt herself warming up. She didn't quite know how to react, or even whether she should. Quite surely these nosey old bats were not trying to tell her how to run her marriage.

"And as you may or may not know, both Geraldine

and I were married for some forty years before our beloveds were called home to glory. So I would think that if anyone was qualified to offer advice regarding the state of marriages, well, wouldn't you say it was us?"

Geraldine nodded.

"'Sides, we don't want it to be said that we didn't take care of our own here at Sweetwater."

Michelle stood there staring at both women. She had heard stories about how they butted into other church members' business, but she had never been the object of one of those discussions until now.

As the women went on about their areas of domestic expertise, Michelle couldn't help but feel like a fool. She was beyond angry at Damien.

"And don't you worry, because we will take care of the other problem. We want to make sure that your spiritually-based counseling has a chance to work." Ms. Geraldine reached over and patted Michelle's shoulder.

"Don't worry 'bout it, baby. No need to thank us just yet. We just want your marriage to be strong and healthy."

"Sure do," Mama Sadie said. "You young women need to lose that 'I can do it all by myself' attitude. Ain't nothing wrong with turning to your elders for help. God didn't put us on this good earth to struggle alone."

Standing there listening to the holy rollers dissect her marriage, Michelle finally admitted that she was at the end of her rope. There was no way she would simply tie another knot and swing, hoping for the best. She had given Damien some of her best years, and she wasn't going to give him anymore.

Now she was about to make him sorry he ever decided to step out on her. Michelle decided that she would put her religion on the shelf momentarily and deal with her wayward husband without putting God first.

CHAPTER 6

Pastor Goodlove was preparing for his weekly session with his masseuse. The stress had been mounting because he was trying to figure out a way to capitalize on his congregation's income tax refunds.

When he finalized the plan, which would bring professional tax experts inside Sweetwater, it was just in time for his massage. He was on the phone with Reginald.

"So, we bring them in, pay them a flat fee, and encourage members to have their taxes done in house," he said.

"You think they're gonna go for that?"

"What? Go for it? You act like I'm trying to sell swampland in Louisiana. Just get the list together and tell them I only need two people."

"Two?" Reginald questioned. "We've got nearly ten thousand members at this church. You think two tax professionals will be able to handle that alone?"

"Look, boy, get two of them here, then tell them

we've got ten assistants who are gonna help," Pastor Goodlove said.

"Assistants? When did we get those?"

"I want you to go over to the accounting and business departments at Texas Southern University and the University of Houston, recruit ten students in all, preferably seniors, and pay 'em about two hundred dollars." When his son didn't answer, Pastor Goodlove looked at the phone.

"Boy, you still there?"

"Um, yeah, Pop. But I don't think that's gonna go over too good. I mean, I know I wouldn't want college kids working on my taxes. I don't understand why we gotta do it this way."

"Look, we gotta do it this way because I say so. Secondly, we aren't telling members they're college students. Boy, tell me you got some of the common sense I raised you with. We call them tax professionals. They will have the refunds directly deposited into the church's bank account. We get our 10 percent off the top, and cut members a check for the balance. We can also offer instant refund loans for a small fee, of course."

Reginald was silent. Pastor Goodlove didn't care. He didn't get to the top by letting what others thought dictate his actions, and he wasn't about to start with his son.

"Make sure you're at least twenty minutes early for our meeting tomorrow. I got some questions about the figures you showed me last time. I need to run. My next appointment is here."

Without waiting for a response from his son, Pastor Goodlove put the phone back in its cradle and smiled when he saw his masseuse. He wanted to pat himself on the back as he thought about all the money the church would take in from the special tax sessions.

As he prepared himself mentally and physically for the masseuse's strong hands, he reminded himself that they needed to assess a special fee for members who needed to file an extension with the IRS.

Damien's eyes were rolling back up into his head. The grand tingling sensation began in the soles of his feet and quickly shot all the way up his legs, to his thighs, and to his member. Jazzlyn was sucking him like she wanted to remove the color from his skin.

"Ooooh, damn, girl. Just damn!"

She cast her gaze upward and looked like she was enjoying the fact that she had the power to make a grown man scream like a baby. But he didn't care. He enjoyed her sweet torture.

When Damien grabbed the sides of her head and tried to move her back, she sucked even harder.

Completely spent, they collapsed next to each other on the bed.

"Whew! You good, girl. You real good," he managed.

"Am I better than your wife?" Jazzlyn asked, elevating herself up onto her elbows.

"C'mon now, Jazz. I told you already, I don't like talking about Chelle. Why you trying to ruin the mood?"

Jazzlyn sucked her teeth.

"Ah, you probably need to get dressed and get ready to go," Damien said as he looked at his watch.

"What's up with that, Dee?" Jazzlyn hissed.

"What?" Damien got up from the bed. "Look, don't tell me you about to start that spend the night shit. I've already told you it ain't gonna happen," he said.

"You know, I'm trying to figure you out. In the beginning, you used to wine and dine me, we'd sneak off to hotels and have a good time. But lately, the last two times we've hooked up, we've come here." Jazzlyn looked around the bedroom. "I mean, what's this supposed to even mean?" she shrugged.

"Deacon Parker will be back soon, so we can't talk about this right now," he said.

"See, that's what I'm talking about, Dee. You starting to treat me like, well, um, like what I've been through before."

Damien rolled his eyes. He wasn't in the mood for Jazzlyn's drama. If he wanted that, he'd stay at home. He quickly got up and walked to the bathroom. When he came back, Jazzlyn was still undressed.

"I mean, you bring me to your friend's house, screw me, then tell me I have to hurry up and go?" Jazzlyn shook her head and shrugged. "I don't even know why I keep doing this to myself. You don't care nothing about me," she sobbed.

He didn't want to, but he walked over to where she stood and took her into his arms. Damien didn't have time for this. He needed Jazzlyn dressed and ready to get out. He didn't want her there when Deacon Parker returned. He hadn't exactly told Deacon what he and Jazzlyn had been doing. Not that Deacon Parker would judge Damien. Deacon Parker himself had talked about his own moments of weakness. And there were tons of them.

"Why don't we go grab a bite to eat? Maybe we could talk about it then. How's that?"

Jazzlyn leaned away from his chest and her eyes lit up.

"Really?"

"Yup, let's get out of here," he suggested.

The smile on her face told him she was probably going to be OK. Jazzlyn rushed to put her clothes back on. She didn't even bother combing her hair.

"OK, I'm ready." She looked at Damien eagerly.

"Cool, let's get out of here."

They were about to step out the front door when Deacon Parker and a ministry member pulled up. He looked at Damien, then at Jazzlyn.

"Oh, Deacon Parker! We're about to go eat. Um, wait, aren't you, ah, Reecey, right?" Jazzlyn looked at the woman.

"I just love to see you and your husband together. I tell myself all the time that I want me a family just like that one—" The hand on Jazzlyn's shoulder made her stop talking. She looked at Damien. "Wwhhaat?" she shrugged.

"Ah, Jazz, we really need to run. Deacon Parker doesn't have time for this." He all but shoved Jazzlyn down the three-step threshold before she could say another word. Deacon Parker grabbed Damien by the arm.

"Got a minute?" he asked.

"Nah, man, I'm um, I really need to get her home. Can it wait?" Damien looked toward Jazzlyn, who was nearly at the car. He glanced at Reecey as if to say, not in front of her.

"I'll call your cell," Deacon Parker said.

Damien rushed off and jumped in the car. He barely waited for Jazzlyn to close her door before he took off and careened around the corner.

For a long while, they didn't speak. Damien started toward Jazzlyn's house.

"I thought we were gonna go eat," she said.

"Um, oh yeah." Damien turned at next corner and pulled into the drive through at the first fast food restaurant he saw. At the speaker, he rolled down his window and looked over at Jazzlyn.

"What do you want?"

She didn't speak.

"OK, you need a sec. Um, I'll take a three piece chicken dinner, spicy, with a large Coke," he said.

When he turned back to Jazzlyn, he noticed tears welling in her eyes.

"What? You not hungry now?" he asked.

"Popeye's drive-through?" Jazzlyn snapped. She shook her head. "We are in Popeye's drive-through!"

"Yeah, and we're holding up the line. What do you want?"

"You cannot be serious!" she screamed. Damien responded by yelling into the speaker.

"That's all. How much?"

The worker gave the total and Damien pulled up to the window to pay. He grabbed his food and pulled back onto the road. By the time he arrived in front of Jazzlyn's apartment complex, half of his meal was eaten.

"You sure you don't want some of this chicken? There's a wing left," he said.

Jazzlyn jumped out of the car, slammed the door, and ran into the gate leading up to her building.

Reginald was sick and tired of his father. But he knew there was nothing he could do about old man Gee. After the phone call, he was not in the mood to do anything else related to the church.

He still couldn't believe he had to drive to Victoria, instead of taking the helicopter. But he was getting his, so he wasn't all that worried.

Reginald Goodlove picked up the phone and dialed the number that was etched in his brain. When the sultry voice answered, he sighed.

"Hey, it's Reggie," he whispered, although he was alone.

"Aeey, big boy. You lookin' for me, huh? What are you in the mood for tonight?"

"I want the supreme," he said.

"Oooohweee, no problem. Should we meet at your place, or you got another address for me?"

"The new Hilton downtown is fine. All night. I'll be there by seven," Reginald said.

"Then we'll be there by six thirty!"

"Cool. Once you arrive and check into our room—you know the number—have at least three bottles waiting. When I knock at the door, answer with a glass of brandy in your hand."

"Sssss, OK, Pappy. What else?"

"Emmh, I want you to wear that black dress. You know the one I like—button down for easy access."

"Yesss, I can do that for you. Anything else, big boy?"

Reginald kept his eyes on the door. He twirled the phone cord around his finger and leaned back in the chair.

"I want to rip the dress open! Then, I want you to sit in my lap for a few minutes and we can share round three. After the first few sips, I want you to kiss me roughly."

"Yes, Pappy, then your hands can travel all over my

body, touch places you've only dreamed about, finger me. Ooooh, wee, then I'll be all wet." Reginald sat up in his chair.

"How wet are we talking?"

"Wet enough for you to guide me onto that massive pole of yours."

Reginald started getting hot. He loosened his tie and reclined in his leather chair again.

"Is it massive or just big?"

"Oh, it's big, Pappy, just the way I like 'em. When you're ready, kiss me again, then I'll spread my legs real, real wide for you," she cooed.

"So you'll be ready to meet your big, hard friend?" he asked, moving his hand down to his crotch.

"Yes, I want to take him into my hands, um, hold and squeeze it . . . sssss, let me wrap my mind around what I'm about to receive. Then, I'll drop to my knees, place a delicate kiss on the head—"

"Where are you gonna kiss it?" Reginald interrupted.

"Right on the head, where you want it. My way of saying hello. When it fully comes to life, um, I'm gonna, uh, I'm sssss, I'm gonna deep throat it . . .'

"Deep throat? Why?" His hand was firmly around his member now.

"'Cause I know that's what you like. I want it to explore the deepest crevasses of my mouth. I wanna feel your juices running down my cheeks."

"And what am I supposed to be doing while you're busy doing this?"

"Um, you are running your fingers through my hair—tugging, pulling—whichever is your pleasure."

"Daaayum, Candy, you sure know what you're doing, huh?"

"Yesssss, Pappy," she breathed.

The loud knock at the door made Reginald jump.

"Uh, hold on a sec," he screamed as he quickly zipped his pants. "Candy, I'll call you back later," he said.

Reginald jumped up and walked to the office, hoping his hard-on had disappeared. He opened his door and stuck his head out.

"Your father, um, I mean Pastor Goodlove wants to see you right away," his secretary said.

"OK, let him know I'm on my way." Reginald quickly shut his door and prayed that the swell between his legs would miraculously go away.

Barry knew he was in over his head. He had put off the emergency call for as long as he could. Now it was time to call in the expert. He sat waiting for his big brother Damien to return his call. If anyone knew how to deal with a crazy woman, quite surely Damien would.

The problem was, it had been two hours since he had last paged his brother, and since then, Sissy had called to ask, more like tell him, she was on her way.

Barry was tired of having to play a willing role in her elaborate plan, but he was helpless when it came to Sissy. She had power over him, and there was very little he could do.

Nearly thirty minutes later, Damien hadn't called, but Sissy stood in front of him. She was naked and demanding.

"Take my nipple into your mouth. Roll it between your teeth, then suck. When you're completely erect,

I just want to sit on it. I don't want you to move. I just want to wiggle my way down," she said.

Barry could hardly believe this was her idea of foreplay. He sat staring up at her. He really didn't want to touch her, but he also knew that if he didn't, she'd use her power to put him in his place. It was like the words of that letter loomed over him each time she was near. He knew to take her threat of exposure seriously. It was a chance he simply couldn't take.

"Well?" Sissy asked. The ring she bought was sparkling on her left ring finger.

Just then, Barry's phone rang. He knew he couldn't move to answer it. A part of him wished he could send out a mental SOS, but that was impossible. Maybe it was his brother, who would rush over since there was no answer.

When Amy's voice rang out through the room, Barry wanted to die. Sissy's head snapped toward the machine, then back at Barry.

"Why is she still calling? I thought I told you to get rid of her!" she snapped.

"Ss-she and her family, they're in Africa. They've been there for three weeks now. I know what you asked me to do, Sissy, but that's gonna take some time. You don't understand the bind you're putting me in," he tried to reason.

"Oh, what I do understand is that you must think I'm some kind of joke, Barry. Pretty soon it's gonna be time for us to set a date. You think I want our church family to think you're some sleazy skirt chaser?"

Sissy stormed off toward the bedroom. Barry knew

he should go after her, but he also knew this would lead to more sex. It was like every time he tried to renew his walk in faith, Sissy came along to help him backslide. He was beyond tired of it, but he knew he had no choice.

He got up from the couch and reluctantly dragged himself toward the back bedroom.

CHAPTER 7

Pastor Goodlove finished his sermon and prepared to escape to his chambers, but thought better of it. He returned to the pulpit. He glanced out at his parishioners.

"It has been brought to my attention that some of you are not taking advantage of the great opportunity we labored to bring your way. As you know, we have set up tax preparation sessions."

"Amen, Pastor!" someone screamed.

"And while some have taken advantage of this, quite a number of you haven't. God said we must be good stewards of the money he has put in our care." He shuffled to one side in front of the pulpit.

"Now, I know you didn't think that money was yours, right? Huh, you know God is just allowing you to use the talents that he bestowed on you so that you may do good, then bring it back to his house." Pastor Goodlove cleared his throat.

"Will a man rob of God?" he asked no one in particular. Members jumped to their feet. It only fueled the pastor's building tempo.

"Ah, I said, will a man rob of God? Yet, you rob me!" He ran to the opposite side of the pulpit. "But you ask, how do we rob you?" the pastor's head snapped in the opposite direction. He lifted one finger to the ceiling. "In tithes and offerings!"

The organ started up again and it was like the Holy Ghost had reemerged. Mama Sadie even did a repeat performance.

Michelle cleared her throat and waited to get the group's attention. She couldn't understand how she was voted to spearhead the annual Purple Tea luncheon.

Sweetwater's Purple Tea luncheon was traditionally held to honor the church's first lady. The issue about whether to hold the annual event had caused deep division among the women of the church.

The first year after Carol Goodlove passed, the Women's Auxiliary decided not to have a luncheon out of respect for her memory. Instead, they had an appreciation breakfast in her honor.

But now, two years after her death and with a new first lady at the helm, many felt it was time to move on with their tradition.

Mama Sadie had been most vocal. She was probably only voicing concerns on behalf of the rest of the holy rollers. She showed up early to the Women's Auxiliary room to have a word with Michelle.

"What if we get news coverage this year? You know that chile is bound to show up in some little hoochie dress. I think we should let that tradition die with the real first lady. This little tramp ain't got no class no how," she had said.

Michelle had closed her eyes and rubbed her temples.

"We took a vote, and most people agreed it was time to move on. Besides, maybe this luncheon will be just the thing to bring Sister Theola into God's—"

"That heathen found herself a bona fide shuga daddy and that's all this is. You know it, I know it, and so does everyone else here at Sweetwater," Mama Sadie snapped, cutting Michelle off.

Shaking her head, Michelle exhaled hard. Why did she have to put up with this foolishness?

"I say we get together and find a way to rid ourselves and the church of that devil." Mama Sadie leaned closer to Michelle. "Now, I just need to know, are you with us or not?"

"Um, what are you saying?" she asked.

"I'm saying that someone has to stand up for the morality of our fine church. We can't have the focus turn to Theola and her sinful ways. It takes away from all the good work we do. Our ministries shouldn't have to take such a hit. And honoring a heathen, well, we just won't have no parts of that."

"Mama Sadie, we're all Christians. Some just aren't as dedicated in their walk with Christ. It just means that those of us who are, need to work a little harder to help our other brothers and sisters," Michelle offered. Mama Sadie got up from her chair, sucked her teeth, and looked at Michelle.

"Chile, please, that's a bunch of mess. No wonder you got some little jezebel running around with your husband. You betta open your eyes, chile." She stormed to the door, pulled it open, then turned back to Michelle. "Oh, and by the way, if you're not with us, then you might as well be against us." Mama Sadie pumped her frail arm toward the ceiling. "I refute the devil and we are on a mission, from God himself, to destroy Lucifer and all of those he employs! Hallelujah!" She walked out and slammed the door behind her.

With so much on her mind, Michelle didn't even feel motivated to go over the agenda, much less try to find a way to honor someone most members despised.

"Ladies, may I have your attention?"

Most people stopped talking and looked toward the front of the room.

Michelle removed the light jacket she wore over her linen dress. Her shoulder length hair was pulled back into a tight bun. Most of her makeup had been selected to cover up the bags beneath her eyes. She couldn't remember the last time she had gotten a good night's sleep.

"OK, so here's where we are so far. The breakfast club will cater the event. We're looking at a menu of chicken and waffles, and fish and grits."

No one commented. Michelle looked up from her notes temporarily. The Women's Auxiliary consisted of twenty board members. With Mama Sadie and the other four holy rollers not present, there were fifteen attending the meeting, including Michelle.

"OK, well if everything is settled, I say we move ahead and get the press release information to the publicity department. So two weeks from now, we'll have the event in the grand ballroom."

Michelle's eyes scanned the room, looking for ideas, questions, or even comments from anyone. When she didn't get any, she shrugged and turned to the table.

"Well, here are the tickets. We're selling them for twenty-five dollars each. Ladies, I thank you and we'll meet again in one week to see how sales are going."

Once the members left the room, Michelle sighed and closed her eyes. She had been planning, and now it was time to begin to execute.

She walked down the hall and looked through the glass door of the meeting room where the deacons were holed up. Michelle made eye contact with her husband and shrugged her shoulders.

He held up both outstretched hands, indicating ten more minutes. She cupped her hand and made a drinking motion.

When Damien nodded, she left to walk across the street. She entered the Starbucks coffee shop and placed an order for two drinks. The Mint Mocha Chip was Damien's favorite.

Before she returned to the meeting room where her husband was, she stopped off at the Women's Auxiliary room.

A few minutes later, Michelle thought, *that should do it*. She listened intently at the door for any sound outside. After building up her courage, she pulled open the door, took a deep breath, and peered outside and down the hall.

When she realized the coast was clear, she stepped out and walked easily back to the room where the deacons were meeting.

A second later, the door swung open and the men, including Damien, rushed out.

"Mint Mocha Chip. Your favorite." She smiled.

"Oh, thanks, babe. You know I got some business I need to handle, right?"

Normally Michelle would be mad, but this time

she extended her own cup toward his, touched it, and sipped.

She watched as he took a large gulp from his flavored coffee.

"Oh, not a problem, hon. I'll see you later this afternoon?"

They turned and started walking toward the front of the church.

"Emm, I might be in late tonight. Depends on what I need to do," he said.

"Ooh?"

"Yeah, but I can try to wrap things up early. Maybe we can take the kids to see a movie or something. I'm not making any promises, but if I make it home early enough," he offered.

"Hmm. Sounds like a plan," she said. Michelle sipped from her cup and watched her husband do the same.

She used her free hand to try to calm her quivering stomach as he drank greedily from the cup.

CHAPTER 8

B and practice was over and Pastor Goodlove was grateful. His head was hurting something terrible. He couldn't wait until their rehearsal room's renovations were complete. He wanted to ask Reginald why he couldn't find a practice room farther away from his office, but his son was missing in action.

As the pastor got up to find his date book, there was a knock on his office door. His assistant, Ms. Geraldine, didn't work after hours, and he usually wasn't disturbed during this time.

"Ah, yeah?" he called toward the door.

"Pastor Goodlove?"

"Yeah?"

"Do you have a moment?"

Pastor Goodlove walked to the door and opened it. The drummer, Maurice Watkins, stood there. The pastor couldn't remember his name, but he knew him.

"Hey, son, what can I do for you?"

"Wondering if you got a moment. Um, I kinda

need to talk to you. You know, um, in private," Maurice said.

"Well, you could call Ms. Geraldine in the morning and set up a counseling appointment," Pastor Goodlove said. Maurice looked down at the floor.

"Um, it's kind of a personal matter," he said.

Pastor Goodlove sighed.

He moved away from the doorway and allowed Maurice into his office. He hoped this wouldn't take long. It wasn't that he was in a hurry to get home to Theola and whatever drama she was dealing with. Pastor Goodlove just had some things on his mind, and they didn't involve counseling some troubled young man. He was thinking about a new investment plan he could share with church members. For a small fee he would let them know about available investment opportunities, like stocks and bonds, but first he had to read up on a few things. He also needed to figure out how much of a fee he could tack on.

The pastor took out his notepad and sat behind his desk.

"Please, sit down," he said.

"Um, thanks!" Maurice sat, but turned to look back at the door that sat slightly ajar.

"Oh, that personal? Feel free to close it," Pastor Goodlove said.

When Maurice returned to his seat, he had a look of uneasiness across his face.

"What is it, son?" Pastor Goodlove noticed for the first time how truly handsome Maurice was. His eyes were round and big, and framed by thick lashes. His narrow nose fit his face handsomely, but it was his smile that was priceless. Maurice smiled nervously.

"I don't really know how to even begin," he admitted.

"Just start at the beginning. But I don't have all night."

"Oh, um, I'm sorry. I keep telling myself, 'Maurice, pull it together, get it together, man.'" He shook his head. "Pastor, I really don't, um. Um, OK, I don't know who else to talk to. I think, um, I think I might be gay, and I'm scared as hell! Ooops! I'm so sorry," Maurice rushed to add. Pastor Goodlove held up his hand.

"No need. Don't even worry about it, Maurice." The pastor looked up at him. "So you believe you are gay? Why?"

Maurice buried his face into his hands. He shook his head.

"I'm, um, I'm almost sure I am. I'm just so scared. I don't know what to do."

"How old are you, Maurice?"

"Pastor, I'm twenty-six and I've been fighting these feelings for a long time. Well, recently I had my first encounter with another man." Maurice fought back tears. "I can't even believe I'm saying this out loud. But, Pastor, I'm a desperate man," he admitted.

"So you recently had relations with another man. How did it, um, I mean, how did you feel?" Pastor shook his own head, searching for the right words. "What I'm trying to say is, how did this make you feel?"

"Guilty, dirty, but confused. It felt good, but I know it's wrong. That's why I've decided to come to you. I was wondering if you could perform an exorcism." Pastor Goodlove swallowed hard.

"A what?"

"You know, an exorcism. I need you to get this evil out of me. Don't worry, Pastor, I'm willing to sign any waiver. I'm willing to do anything you want. I just need to get this out of my system. I need you to heal me, Pastor." Maurice began to sob uncontrollably.

A frown creased Pastor Goodlove's forehead.

Maurice's sobs soon turned to gut-wrenching wails. Pastor Goodlove walked to the other side of his desk and took Maurice into his arms.

When the pastor felt Maurice's shoulders convulse against his chest, he had to fight to control the fire burning deep inside his own loins.

"Ooooh, yesss, Damien. I want to feel you until it's way up in me, as far as it'll go," Gina cried.

"Oh, baby, is it good for you?" he breathed.

"Yeeesss. It's good. You feel me, baby? Move it around, let it get comfortable in there. I want you to leave your mark in there."

The more she talked, the harder Damien pumped.

"Make me call your name, just make me," she cried

"Oh yeah, girl, you got some real good pussy."

All of a sudden, she stopped moving with him.

"Wwwhat's wrong?" Damien slowed his pace, but didn't stop.

"Um, I wanna ride. I know you noticed I'm about to cum. I want to stretch it. I've been wanting you for way too long to just give in like this." Damien stopped and rolled off Gina.

"Go'n then, girl. Do your thang. Ride big daddy if that's what you want to do." As she climbed on top of him, he slapped her ass with his open palm. "Say, why don't you turn around, grab my ankles, and lemme see that beautiful ass of yours while you pony up!"

She did what she was told. She turned her body, with her back and ass facing Damien.

"That's right, big daddy. Take it the way you want it. Do me hard, do me rough, do me like you're trying to get me sprung. Don't hold back. Tear it up!"

He spread his legs and she grabbed them with her hands. He spread them even wider.

"You feel it, girl?" Damien asked as his eyes rolled up into the back of his head.

After a few minutes of intense body slapping, Gina humped him harder, then squeezed her walls tighter around him. "Sssss . . . yes Big Daddy. She clawed at his legs and ankles, gripping him harder. Suddenly her body jerked, her eyes widened, and her back arched. She stopped moving again.

"Damn, what's wrong now?" Damien hissed.

"We gotta switch. I'm about to cum," she said.

"Well, that's what we here for, huh?" Damien was starting to get frustrated. He wanted to bust a nut and couldn't because every time he got going good, she'd stop and insist they switch up. Gina was breathing hard.

"OK, flip me over and take it from the back. Then you can whisper in my ear. Um, you know, tell me how good it is."

Damien got on his knees behind Gina's round behind. All the damn talking was killing his mood until he realized he was about to do it doggie-style—his favorite position.

"OK, when you're finally about to explode, grab my breasts and squeeze them while you cum," Gina instructed.

"Look, baby, you got yourself a man here. I don't need any instructions. I just need you to let me do my thang. You just hold on and enjoy the ride, cool?"

"Well, I just know what I like," Gina said. "Here, touch my tits. Run your fingers through my hair," she managed to say before Damien reached up and used his hand to turn her head toward the wall.

"Yeah, that's it. You hitting my spot. Damn, Damien, I knew you were as good as they said," Gina huffed. Damien stopped.

"What did you say?" Gina looked back at him.

"I said I knew you were as good as they said."

"Who's been talking about me?"

Gina slapped his hand that was resting on her hip.

"Ah, this is not the time. You're kinda in the middle of something here. We can talk about that later."

Damien knew she was right. He started moving his hips, slowly at first, then he picked up momentum. Soon he and Gina were matching each other's rhythm.

BOOM! BOOM!

"What the fuck?" Damien screamed. Gina collapsed onto the bed.

"Is that someone at the door? Somebody know you're here?" she asked.

"Ssssh, let's just be quiet. Come here. I was almost there."

BOOM! BOOM!

"Damien, I know you're in there. Open up this fucking door now!"

"Oh, shit!" Gina jumped up from the bed and

grabbed her clothes off the floor. "Damn, is that your wife?" she cried as she rushed toward the bathroom.

Damien didn't know quite what to do. How the hell did Michelle even find him? *This can not be happening!* he thought as he paced the floor.

He heard Gina in the bathroom cursing up a storm. His heart was beating so hard and fast that he thought surely he'd soon see his maker. Suddenly, the bathroom door flung open and Gina stood there looking at Damien.

"What are you gonna do about this? I can't lose my family over you!" She slapped her forehead. "You screw everybody in church for years, and the minute I try to get me a little, we get caught. Now ain't this some shit! I knew I should've left your hoing ass alone! Damn," she huffed.

BOOM! BOOM!

"You betta open this door. I swear I'ma call the police. Who in there with you? Don't even try to act like you don't hear me, Deacon Damien Goodlove! I know you in there, and whoever that bitch is, I'm about to whup her ass!"

That's when Damien stopped and looked toward the door.

"Jazzlyn?" he called toward the closed door.

"Um, yeah," she answered. Gina looked at Damien, then toward the door.

"Who the fuck is Jazzlyn? Your wife's name is Michelle." Damien shook his head.

"I know you didn't fuck that skank from Wilshire Baptist," Gina said. Damien put his hand up to hush her.

"You need to quit. Don't worry about who I've been fucking," he said.

"Oh, I need to worry if you been screwing her. Shit, everybody knows her pussy got so many miles on it, I'm surprised you still fit in there."

Damien ignored Gina, walked to the door, and opened it.

"What the fuck is wrong with you? Why you out here acting the straight ghetto fool?" Jazzlyn kept looking over his shoulder.

"Who in here with you? Don't even try to lie. I smell that stank ho!"

"I know you didn't call me a ho!" Gina rushed toward Jazzlyn. Jazzlyn stepped back and looked at Damien and Gina.

"Oh my, you're screwing Deacon Collier's wife? Man, you really are a dog, huh?"

"Bitch, don't worry about who I am. What are you doing here anyway?"

She looked at Damien and smiled.

"You gonna tell her why I know how to find you here, or you want me to tell her?"

Damien stumbled. A pain shot through his eye and toward his temple. When his legs buckled, the women stopped arguing and looked at him.

"What's your problem?" Jazzlyn asked.

"Um, I'm cool." Damien sat on the bed. "Look, why don't y'all both take that shit outside? I ain't in the mood for this right now." He suddenly felt light-headed.

This had been happening quite frequently lately, but he didn't have time to think about that. Gina looked at him.

"Thanks for nothing!" she snapped. She looked at Jazzlyn on her way out. "I wish you would mention this to anyone. I'll beat your nasty ass down like a runaway slave," she spat.

When Reginald left his father's office, his head was hanging low and he felt like shit. He had no idea why he let the old man get to him that way.

He'd stopped by his office, but not for long. He had one phone call to make, and then he was on his way to paradise. He dialed the number from memory. When the sexy voice answered, he turned to face his office door.

"Hey, Candy, it's Reggie."

"Emmmm, I was just thinking about you, babe," she cooed.

"Great, um, you think you could meet me for a few hours?" Reginald ran his hand over his head. "You know, at the regular place."

"The suite?" Candy asked gleefully.

"You know how I do it. Meet me there in an hour?"

"I'll be there. But oh, Reggie, you want me to spend the night? If so, you know that's gonna be extra, right? And you can't give me a tip, then say, use that to make up the difference. Agreed?"

"Candy, I know you not trying to call me cheap, right?"

"Sssss, no, Pappy, I wouldn't do that. I just needed to make it clear. Hey, I can get in trouble if my money isn't straight. I'm just a working girl."

"Yeah, look, Candy, I've had a hard day. I didn't mean nothing by it. Say, you know what, why don't we just plan to stay there for two days? You think you can handle that?"

"I sure can." She giggled. "I'm gonna see if we

can't cut you some slack for the two days. I mean, you are one of our most loyal customers."

"Cool. See you in an hour," he said.

Reginald told himself not to worry about the more than ten thousand dollars he spent a month at Centerfolds, an exclusive escort service. He didn't even miss being married.

After being divorced for seven years, he had finally grown accustomed to his new life. His ex-wife Maria quickly walked out on him after she said she couldn't take it anymore.

At times he remembered it like it had happened just yesterday.

"You are a fool to stay in this mess. The man is crazy. He ain't gon do nothing but run you down, and I can't stay with no man who can't even stand up to his own damn daddy!" Maria had screamed as she packed her bags.

That rainy day in May, Reginald stood at the door to their bedroom watching as his wife packed all of her belongings.

"I'm tired of this shit. You guys, all of you Goodlove men, are nothing but crooks. Yeah, old man Gee keeps getting rich, but at what expense to the rest of us? Your mama got her head buried in the sand, then the other two of your brothers can't even have an independent thought of their own. I did not sign up for this. Then he think he can just talk to me like I'm nobody? Oh hell no, I'm out!"

He still only looked on.

"And you didn't say a single word when he disrespected me! The man had the audacity to tell me that I'd better be happy he gave the green light or you wouldn't be with someone like me?" She stopped her packing to point toward her chest. "What the hell did he think I was gonna do—what the rest of you do? I don't have to sit there and eat shit just because none of you have the balls to stand up to your old man. You're spineless, and I'm tired!"

The image of Candy's ripe breasts and round behind jarred him back to the mission at hand. He hung up the phone and rushed out of the office.

Reginald prayed to himself that he'd be able to get out of the building before his father came beckoning.

He couldn't wait to get his hands on Candy. And if she did a real good job, he planned to give her an extra sweet bonus.

When he pulled out of the parking lot he was so thrilled he could hardly keep his mind on the road. Candy knew how to make him feel like a real man.

She didn't yell or scream unless they were in the throes of passion and he was wearing her out. When he called, she dropped whatever she was doing and gave him phone sex, or any kind of attention he needed. When they were together, she sexed him until he couldn't take it anymore. He didn't need a wife as long as he could keep the money flowing. And he planned to do just that.

Before he hopped on Highway 59 toward downtown, he walked into the nearest Washington Mutual Bank.

He liked walking into that particular branch. People treated him well. Despite the line that curved nearly out of the door, the manager walked out of his office when he saw Reginald.

"Mister Goodlove, how are you today?"

They shook hands.

"Here to make a deposit or withdrawl?"

Reginald glanced around the crowded bank. The manager quickly ushered him toward his office.

That's when Reginald pulled out and presented the check for twenty-five thousand dollars.

"I need that in large bills, please."

The manager looked down at the check and smiled up at Reginald.

"Of course."

Every time Barry fornicated he felt like the bottom of a shoe. He knew it was wrong, but Sissy had him by the balls, literally. And anytime he acted like he didn't want to do whatever she wanted, she reminded him of what she had said in the letter. Barry was curious about whether she really had the tape. But then he told himself there was no way she'd know details of what was on the tape if she hadn't at least seen it. Either way, he didn't want to upset her. While he knew he was wrong for fornicating, there was a constant battle brewing inside him.

It was wrong, but it felt so very good. He sat on the edge of the bed, his eyes closed, and his hands covering his face. He heard Sissy before he opened his eyes, and he looked up at her.

"So, tell me what you enjoyed most, then tell me when we're gonna do it again," Sissy said.

"You know I don't like doing this," Barry said.

"Emph, that's what your mouth says now, but about twenty minutes ago, I couldn't tell you weren't having a good time," she snickered.

"Why do you keep doing this?" he asked.

"Doing what?" Sissy sat next to Barry and rubbed his shoulders. "Did you tell Amy yet?"

Barry's heart froze. If he told the truth, Sissy would get all worked up again. If he lied, she'd want more details. How did his life end up this way? He was so angry at himself sometimes, that he didn't know what to do.

"OK, let's try this again. I said, have you told Amy yet?" Barry turned to her.

"Sissy, they're not back yet. I told you they went to Africa for a month."

"Hmmm."

Barry looked away from her.

"All I know is when that little tramp gets back, I want to be there when you break the news to her."

"I'm not gonna do that," Barry said.

"What? What do you mean you're not gonna do that? You should be willing to do whatever I want. I'm your future wife."

"Where's your heart?"

"You've got it, babe." She softened a bit. Barry shook his head.

"If you had a heart, you'd respect the fact that I love another woman," he said gently. When Sissy didn't have a natural fit, he continued cautiously.

"I think you're a fine person, Sissy, I really do, but why would you want to marry someone who doesn't really love you back?" Barry stopped speaking when his voice cracked a bit.

She dropped to her knees and pulled his legs wider apart. She squeezed herself between them and took his face into her hands. Sissy looked him straight in his eyes.

"Because I know what we're capable of. You can and will learn to love me. You just don't know it yet, but you've gotta trust me."

"So am I just supposed to forget about Amy? Don't you mind me being with you because you forced me to? And what about my heart? What am I supposed to do?"

"Give it time. Give us time," she whispered.

"What if I don't want to?"

Sissy fell back onto her butt. She sat there and stared at Barry. A look washed over her face that sent chills running through his veins. He wondered what she was thinking, what was on her mind. It didn't take long for him to find out.

CHAPTER 9

"I said, uh, don't allow the hell that exists around you," Pastor Goodlove waved his arms around his body, "to get in you!"

"Speak, Pastor, speak!" voices screamed.

"You see, whenever you decide to live the way you want to, God will definitely deal with you!" Pastor Goodlove pointed his finger toward members of the congregation.

"Hallelujah! Pastor, hallelujah!" the crowd cried feverishly.

"He's a mighty, mighty God!" Pastor Goodlove jumped up and down a few times. His large frame moved with its usual grace.

Mama Sadie was on her feet, and she started screaming.

"I saaaid, heeello somebody!" Pastor Goodlove used his hand to cup his ear. "I saaaid, heeello somebody!" He ran to the opposite side of the pulpit.

"When God looks at you, what does he see?" People extended their arms toward the ceiling and began swaying.

"When you decide to live contrary to God's will, there's going to be hell to pay!"

Mama Sadie flung her body from side to side, threw her arms to the ceiling, and started screaming. She jumped up and down.

"Hello, somebody! I saaaid, you, you, you, and you," Pastor Goodlove hollered as he moved across the front of the pulpit and pointed at various faces.

"You all must maintain your Christ-like character in a contrary community." The organ player's beat started off slow, then built up and matched each step the pastor took, building up to the normal, triumphant harmony.

"God can help you," he pointed at someone, "and you, and you too, and even me!" With his head flung back and his eyes closed tightly, Pastor Goodlove's chant turned into song. "I saaaid, heeello, somebody!" Pastor Goodlove screamed louder.

Pastor Goodlove watched as a calm came over the congregation. When he thought the moment was appropriate, he began again.

"I want to say thank you for your faith. I'm glad to report that 98 percent of you took advantage of our tax help program. We'd like to announce that before the extension deadline of April 15th, we'll invite a few tax professionals back to assist those of you who procrastinated." He cleared his throat. "I'd also like to take this moment to welcome the visitors who have joined us here at Sweetwater today. Please stand." The pastor's eyes scanned the crowd. "I said, I need all of the visitors to stand and be recognized."

Members began looking around the church. This was not part of his normal program. Soon members began whispering among themselves. Mama Sadie had even stopped her reaction to the Holy Ghost's usual visit.

"OK, well, Sweetwater, I want to introduce you all to a very special visitor who seems to want to go unrecognized." Pastor Goodlove walked halfway up the aisle.

"Let's give a warm Sweetwater welcome to Trent Norwood." Trent stood, then quickly sat back down. "See, Trent is modest, but he's very important to your pastor. Trent is my massage therapist. He's responsible for taking the knots and stress out of your pastor's shoulders."

Members reached over, hugged Trent, and shook his hand. Pastor Goodlove looked at his watch.

"As a matter of fact, after the word today, I might need Trent's magic fingers."

That comment gave way to several chuckles as the assistant pastors stepped forward for tithes and offerings.

Nearly two hours after service, Pastor Goodlove was locking his office door as Trent stepped inside. The Pastor was ready to be on the receiving end of a special kind of healing.

Theola noticed the little punk as she rushed down the hall away from her husband's chambers. She was about to get on a plane and go to Jamaica or the Keys. She was sick and tired of the church, its members, and ole Gee himself.

She only wished she had someone to go with, but since she didn't, she figured she'd go spend her husband's money, get drunk, and find a young Jamaican to ruin.

But before she could escape Sweetwater, she saw Michelle sitting in her car. Theola told herself to just leave. It was none of her business that her daughter-in-law was sitting there crying her eyes out.

Theola walked over to her BMW, hit the keyless entry, and opened her door. She tossed her Louis Vuitton bag inside, then slammed the door shut.

Against her better judgment, she walked over to Michelle's car and softly tapped on the window. When Michelle looked up, her eyes were bloodshot red. A small part of Theola hoped that Michelle wouldn't lower the window, but she knew better. Misery loved company. When Michelle used a button to lower the window, Theola looked around the parking lot.

"You wanna go somewhere and um, have a drink? Um, I dunno, maybe we could talk or something. You look like you could use a friend." Michelle didn't know what to say or do.

"Um, I don't really drink, Theola." Michelle sniffled. Theola shrugged her shoulders.

"Well, OK then. I was just thinking you might need someone to talk to. Ain't no sweat off me," she said. Before Michelle could roll the window back up, Theola turned and started back toward her own car.

"Wait, Theola," Michelle screamed. She looked out of the side mirror.

When Theola stopped and turned around, Michelle was out of the car and walking toward her.

"Emmm, what about Ninfa's? I love their Margaritas."

"Girl, which one?" Theola screamed.

"What about the one on Westheimer, you know, far enough away from prying eyes." Michelle smiled.

"I know exactly where it is," Theola said.

An hour later, they were on their second pitcher of strawberry Margaritas.

"So why were you crying in the parking lot?" Theola asked. She sipped her drink.

The smile faded from Michelle's face, and Theola was suddenly sorry she even mentioned it. She put her hand up.

"You know what, we don't even have to talk about that. I'm just glad to have someone to spend some time with."

Instead of responding, Michelle dug deep into her Coach duffle bag. She pulled out a stack of pictures and tossed them onto the bar.

Theola nearly spit out her drink. Her eyes widened in horror. She picked up a few of the pictures and her mouth dropped.

"Jesus!" She started flipping through the pictures. "What are these?" she asked.

"Um, pictures of naked women," Michelle said easily.

"I can see that much," Theola said, still glancing at the pictures. "Ooooh, this one is really wrong for those cottage cheese thighs. And look at her droopy titties. Girl, I'd pay somebody to fix mine if they looked like this. Where the hell did you get these?"

"My husband's glove compartment. I also found his stash of condoms."

"Damn! That's deep. Hmm, you're taking it well."

"Oh, trust that's because I got something for his ass."

CHAPTER 10

Pastor Goodlove felt better than words could express. He lay stretched out on the sofa with his body in a complete state of relaxation. Despite the fact that nearly thirty minutes had passed since he experienced the very best orgasm of his life, he was still basking in its afterglow. Just when he was about to get up and change clothes, there was a knock on his office door.

"Damn, isn't everyone gone?" he mumbled.

He got up and went to the door. Without asking who was there, he swung the door open to find Maurice standing there.

"Um, Pastor, am I disturbing you?" he asked.

"No, not at all. Why don't you step inside?"

Pastor Goodlove looked down the hall in both directions, then closed and locked the door behind Maurice.

"So, how are you?" he asked before walking around to his large leather chair.

"Well, Pastor, um, that's kind of why I'm here. I

need to speak to you." Maurice picked at his fingers and didn't quite look Pastor Goodlove in the eyes.

"It's like I told you before, Maurice, struggling with your sexuality isn't something that's cured overnight." Pastor shook his head, giving his words time to settle. "As we've discussed, an exorcist deals with abstracting the devil, evil. If I felt it would be beneficial to you, I would recommend someone, but I don't believe it is in this case."

"I understand, but that's not what I wanted to talk to you about this time." Maurice looked up.

"Oh, I'm sorry. I guess I jumped the gun a bit." Pastor Goodlove chuckled. "I'm sorry about that. Why don't I just be quiet and let you talk for a moment."

"Well, um, what I'm trying to say is, um . . ." Maurice started picking at his fingers again. "I, um, well, when I came to you last time, I came to you for help. And well, what happened—"

Pastor Goodlove opened the drawer and pulled out his checkbook. He flipped it open until he found a blank check. Before Maurice could utter another word, Pastor Goodlove pushed his pen and looked up at him.

"So, you need a little help is what you're saying?"

Maurice looked puzzled. His eyebrows knitted together.

"Help?" he asked back.

"Well, I know you're going through some things, and I thought maybe a few dollars might help. You know, you could take a trip, buy some new clothes— do some things you just haven't been able to." The pastor shrugged.

"Um, yeah, I guess that would be nice," Maurice said.

Pastor Goodlove pushed the check toward him. When Maurice picked up the check, the pastor stood.

"All right then. I'd like to sit and chat, but I'm due in Beaumont in less than two hours, and I have no idea where the helicopter pilot is." The pastor laughed.

Maurice rose from his chair, then stumbled back down when he looked at the check. His hands began to tremble. Pastor Goodlove wasn't in the mood, but tried to hide the sour expression which had made its way to his face.

"You OK?" he asked.

"Um, pastor, ah, this check—" Maurice began. Pastor Goodlove started back toward his desk. He was prepared to go up another five, or even ten if he thought it would help.

"What, you need a little more? Here, let me have it." But when he reached for the check, Maurice snatched it back.

"Pastor, I just wanted to make sure you didn't make a mistake. I thought maybe you wrote too many zeros."

"Oh." Pastor Goodlove walked back toward the door. "No, son, ten thousand dollars is the least I can do for you, considering what you've done for me."

Damien was beside himself. With his arms hugging the toilet in his bathroom at home, he thought he would die if he puked one more time. He couldn't believe he had plans to spend the next two days fucking, drinking, and gambling, and instead he was sick and stuck at home.

Chances are, he'd have to cancel his date with that new honey he'd picked up a few weeks ago. He told himself he was through with both Jazzlyn and Gina.

But now he wondered where the hell his wife was. He kept telling himself he'd call for an ambulance if he threw up one more time, especially if she didn't come home. He was already running a fever and things weren't getting any better.

Damien knew he hadn't eaten anything unusual, so he was baffled. Sure he had finished off his prized bottle of Remy Martin that he'd been sipping on for the past three days, but he didn't have enough for a hangover. That was the good stuff, so rarely did it leave him with any symptoms of overdrinking, especially a hangover.

Besides, he had endured enough of those to know that they didn't come with a fever. Damien knew something was seriously wrong when he felt as if his skin had been set ablaze. Even the spaces between his fingers and toes were on fire.

When he simply couldn't stand the heat anymore, he finally broke down, mustered up the strength to pick up the phone, and dialed 9-1-1.

Hours later, a doctor in the emergency room pulled a curtain around his bed for privacy.

"Mr. Goodlove, we still have not been able to get in touch with your wife. Your father is out of town, but we did reach your brother Barry. However, I wanted to tell you, this is just as we suspected. What do you know about the substance warfarin?" Damien eased his body up on the bed.

"Ah, not much, what is it?"

"It's a main ingredient in rat or rodent poison. Emm, like d-CON, it contains warfarin. In humans, it basically prevents the blood from clotting and can cause internal bleeding, depending on how much you have ingested. I'd like to run additional tests, so we'll be admitting you. We'll start you on vitamin K."

"So, doc, are you saying I somehow ingested rat poison? There's got to be some kind of mistake." The doctor looked at Damien.

"The tests prove otherwise. Sorry, I know this is probably upsetting, but we can't dispute the findings. All of the tests came back positive."

"So you're saying I was poisoned? Wouldn't I have known if someone tried to feed me rat poison? I mean the warfarin, I should've tasted it, huh?" Damien was beside himself. The saddest part was that he didn't know who to blame. It could've been any of the four or five women he was sleeping with at the same time.

Considering what the doctor had said, he was grateful they couldn't find Michelle. How the hell would he explain to her that someone had tried to poison him?

"Well, not at all. Warfarin is odorless and tasteless. Based on your symptoms, I'd say you may have been ingesting it in small doses." The doctor touched Damien's shoulder. "It's OK, buddy, we'll get you feeling better. But you need to try to figure out who would want you dead."

By the time the doctor disappeared behind the curtain, Damien's mouth and eyes were still hanging wide open.

"Hhmmmmm, I don't know." Sissy held her manicured fingertip between her glossy lips. "There's something about this one that just makes me look real, real good." Sissy turned to get a better look at her reflection. She used her hands to smooth out the contours of the dress from her chest to her thighs. She knew Barry would like her in this dress.

"Well, as you can see, the satin sheath has a draping effect. The sweeping train has crystal beading and a cascading effect." The saleswoman finished her pitch with a sweeping motion over the train that was attached to the back of the dress. "Most of the customers who try this one on say that they feel like Cinderella in it. And I don't have to tell you why. It's an absolutely gorgeous dress."

"I can see," Sissy agreed. "You don't think I'm too busty for this, do you?" Sissy cupped the front of her dress with her hands. "I mean, I don't want to look X-rated on my wedding day."

"Well, I usually recommend the halter design for our top heavy customers. But I do have to admit, this is just breathtaking," the saleswoman said. "This is certainly a showstopper."

This was Sissy's very last fitting at the David's Bridal store. The dress would be ready in time for her and Barry's ceremony.

Barry hadn't exactly said when he wanted to get married, but she knew he'd want her to keep it simple, so she had. Her mother Julia was flying in from Columbus, Ohio, as was a cousin she used to be close with.

Her cousin Brandi agreed to stand up for her as a bridesmaid and maid of honor. The ceremony was going to be held at Sweetwater. Barry didn't have to worry. He also didn't have to tell her to handle everything.

The moment she bought her ring, she knew exactly where they'd get married, and where they'd go for a honeymoon. Besides, Sissy knew Barry was the type who just needed to be told when and where to show up.

It had been Sissy who set up the fitting for him, his brother, and his cousin Wayne. She didn't mind doing all of the legwork one bit. She told herself that the only way a girl could truly make sure her wedding day was perfect was by doing everything herself. Sissy had hand selected the wedding planner and told her she needed a classy wedding in record time. So far things were falling into place quite nicely.

"Where are y'all getting married?" the saleswoman asked.

"Oh, at Sweetwater Powerhouse of God."

"What a nice selection. I've heard about it, but never been," she said.

"Well, it's beautiful. It's in the heart of Sugarland, with a lake and a gazebo in the back. You know how beautiful it is in that area."

"Yeah, it is real nice down there."

"We're staying in that new hotel out in First Colony after the reception. They have a honeymoon suite with its own private balcony."

"Wow, sounds nice," the saleswoman said. "So do you want to try the tank dress?"

"I think I should. I mean, it's not too late for me to change my mind if the tank fits better, is it?" Sissy asked.

"Not at all. Here, let me go get one in your size. I'll meet you in the fitting room."

When the saleswoman left, Sissy turned several

times and looked at herself in the mirror. She inhaled, released her breath, and tried to imagine the look on Barry's face when he laid eyes on his lovely bride.

Snapping out of it, she grabbed the dress by both sides and made her way to the dressing room. Within minutes, the saleswoman had three tank-style dresses for her to try on.

Sissy stepped out to the three-way mirror wearing selection number two.

"I think we've found *the* dress," the saleswoman declared.

When Sissy looked at her reflection, her mouth dropped. She began to tremble.

"OHMIGOD! This is it!" she exclaimed. "This is the one."

"And by the looks of it, you'll need very few alterations. The fit is close to perfect."

"How long will it take for this to be ready?"

"You could use a slight hem, so we can have this done in two days." The saleswoman walked around Sissy as she stood in front of the mirror on the platform. "Maybe by tomorrow evening," the woman whispered.

"That would be perfect." Sissy giggled.

Finally, everything was in place—the dress, the location, the rings, the guest list—and Sissy had single-handedly done it all.

She couldn't wait to let Barry know everything was complete. So what if they hadn't spoken since that awkward moment at his house a couple of weeks ago? Quite surely Amy and her snooty family were back, and maybe he was still trying to help her get over the heartache,

Sissy figured Barry would need the time to clear

his head anyway, after the devastation he had to deliver to Ms. Perfect Little Amy. So instead, Sissy delved into the wedding plans. Yeah, they were separated, and he hadn't returned any of her calls, but still, Sissy figured it would do little good to push him. She was accustomed to waiting for what she really wanted, so this would be no different as far as she was concerned.

She told herself she'd wait until she finalized everything for their wedding, then go to him. She'd say she was sorry for acting so silly and insecure. They'd kiss, have passionate make-up sex, and then get ready for their wedding day.

Sissy was so proud of herself as she drove home that she couldn't stop thinking about the fact that she would eventually be Mrs. Barry Goodlove. Finally, all of her hard work had paid off. She had won, just like she knew she would.

When she arrived home, she decided to call Barry one more time. He picked up on the first ring.

"You must've been expecting my call," she sang into the phone.

"Um, what's up?"

What's up? Sissy thought that was a strange greeting.

"Barry, babe, I wanted to let you know that the wedding is all set. All we have to do is sit down and pick a date. I guess we should do that with your dad . . . find out when he's free."

"Um, I gotta go!"

Sissy couldn't believe it when she heard the dial tone ringing loudly in her ear.

CHAPTER 11

"The only reason you love like you do . . ." Pastor Goodlove slid across the small platform that the pulpit stood on. "I said, the only reason you love like you love, and praise the way you praise, is because you've been through the storm!"

"Amen, Pastor! Amen!" someone yelled.

"Hallelujah!"

"When you make it to the mountain top, huh, you better understand God was the one steering you!"

"Preach, Pastor! Preach!"

"I said, if you think you did it alone, think you made that move by your own talent and skills . . . huh, well, I gotta tell you something!"

"What, Pastor! What you gotta tell me?" a woman's voice screamed.

"I gotta tell you," Pastor Goodlove paused for dramatic effect. He walked from behind the pulpit. "I said, I gotta tell you, when you make it out of the flood, survive the storm, you better recognize. Better yet, you better drop to your knees, build an altar, and praise him!"

The music began, the fans were flapping, and the saints were on their feet.

Just as the pastor was about to take off to his chambers, two white men approached the pulpit.

"Are you the Reverend Ethan Ezeekel Goodlove the third?" one of the white men asked amid the jubilee. Frowning, the pastor sized them up.

"Ah, yes." The quiet man shoved a large envelope toward the pastor.

"You've been served," he said. Before the pastor or anyone else could react, the men turned and ran from the church.

Pastor Goodlove was a bit baffled, but not enough to be worried about the contents of the envelope. As one of his assistants prepared for tithes and offerings, he dropped the envelope on Reginald's lap and dashed to his office.

After church, Michelle was using the restroom when she heard the mumbling. She sat as still as she could in the stall, realizing the gossipers probably cared nothing about being overheard.

"I just don't believe it. I won't. I know people had issues when the pastor married that younger woman, but ain't no way in the world anyone can make me believe that about my pastor. He does too much good."

"So, because someone does good, you don't think them capable of taking advantage of someone else? I mean, think about it. Pastor Goodlove is a powerful, rich man. Sometimes they tend to think they can have anything they want. Some of 'em even think they're above the law," the second voice said.

Michelle heard the water running.

"Yeah, I know what you're saying, but we're talking about homosexuality. He's a man of God. Ain't no way. Besides, I remember when my mama had to have that heart surgery and her insurance wouldn't cover the entire cost. Guess who stepped up, wrote the check, and didn't ask any questions? Hmm, he didn't even bat an eye."

"Yeah, I remember that."

"Girl, that was like fifty thousand dollars."

"That still don't mean he didn't do it."

Michelle heard them pull paper towels. When the door closed and she was confident they were gone, she emerged from the stall.

"What the hell is going on?" she asked her reflection.

She needed to catch up with Kim and Tammy. If anyone was on top of church gossip, it was those two. She rushed to leave church after thanking her parents for keeping the girls. She had explained to her mother that she and Damien needed some alone time. The girls had been with their grandparents for two weeks. Michelle told herself that she didn't want her girls around when she began her quest for revenge.

It had been three days since she'd last seen her husband. She called his cell phone until his voicemail was overflowing. No one had seen nor heard from him, and he didn't even show up for church. Michelle figured he was off with another one of his little tramps.

Over brunch she was waiting for Tammy to answer her questions. When Tammy acted like she didn't want to talk, Michelle rolled her eyes.

"Why are y'all acting all funny? What did you hear?" she asked again.

"Tell her, shit," Kim said.

"Well, some people are saying that your father-in-law is accused of sexual assault. Remember when those two white guys came into church right after the pastor's sermon? Well, they served him with a lawsuit. Word is, he's being sued for trying to rape a church member, a member of the band, girl."

"What?" Michelle was shocked. Her mind quickly tried to think of any of the women who were capable of making the accusation. Probably some gold digger looking for a quick and easy payday.

"Wait, let me guess, is it that little soprano?" Michelle asked. "You know the one. She's always looking at Theola funny."

"Girl, that's just about everyone except you lately, but later for that. Girl, the pastor ain't being sued by a woman. He's being sued by Maurice, you know, the drummer!"

Damien had been hanging out at his youngest brother's apartment. He hadn't talked to his wife, his kids, his girlfriends, or even his father. He still couldn't believe someone wanted him dead. And as far as he was concerned, all of the previously mentioned, except the kids, were suspect.

He remembered when he was in the hospital, alone. As he sat up waiting for the doctor to sign his release papers, he wished for someone by his side.

But as badly as he had treated women, he wasn't surprised that he didn't know who was trying to kill him, or even who he could call.

The doctor walked in and sat on a stool with wheels.

"OK, Mr. Goodlove, you look great. I have a few papers for you to sign. You need to pick up your prescription, and remember to call if you have any problems. The internal bleeding was caught early enough, so you didn't have any problems with clotting."

Damien signed where he was instructed and looked back at the doctor.

"Is there something else?" the doctor asked.

"I guess not. Um, well there is sort of. So someone really tried to poison me?"

Just then, the door swung open and Barry stepped into the room.

"Hey," he said.

"Oh, that's my brother. Go ahead," Damien instructed the doctor.

"OK, well, yes. And in a situation like this, we're legally obligated to notify the authorities. Your information has been passed along to HPD. I guess because your case wasn't severe, they'll probably send an officer to your home or even ask you to come downtown."

"An officer?" Damien asked. "You mean somebody could go to jail?"

"That would ultimately be up to the district attorney, but yes, this could've been very serious. I'm glad you came in when you did. What if you thought you just had a cold or the flu even? It's not unusual to have the flu in the spring."

"I could've died," Damien said more than asked.

"Yes, you could have died. But that's in the past

now. Once you take that medication for seven days, you should be as good as new." The doctor chuckled.

His lighthearted approach did very little to ease Damien's mind about the culprit. Sure, Jazzlyn's name popped up, but lately, Damien was reevaluating all he thought he knew about his string of women, and friends even. It could've easily been Michelle who tried to poison him. *Nah, no way*, he thought.

When Damien was released, Barry drove him home. He knew Michelle was at work. Damien felt like a stranger in his own home. He aimlessly walked from the living room to the kitchen to the bedroom. With each step he wondered whether Michelle had poisoned him in his own home.

Part of the problem was the fact that he didn't know who to point the finger at. He had no idea. Damien strolled into the room he used as a study and glanced around. There were stacks of papers and pictures of his family in happier times, before he started straying from home.

Now, he was spending most of his time away from his house and at Barry's place. When his brother walked into the living room, Damien snapped out of his memories.

"I asked if you needed anything," Barry said.

"Oh, my bad. Sorry, my mind is gone, man. But, nah, I'm good."

Barry sat on his sofa and sighed long and hard.

"You OK?" Damien asked. "You act like you're the one who got poisoned and damn near died."

Barry stared at his brother, but didn't say anything at first.

"What are you gonna do, man?" Barry asked.

Damien shook his head. He had no idea.

"I still can't believe someone wanted me dead!"

"Yeah, that's something!" Barry glanced beyond Damien. "You know you can stay here for as long as you need to, but you can't hide forever."

"I know. I just need to try to figure out my next move. I mean, it's not like I can waltz through the door and say, 'Hey, Michelle, honey, did you slip me some rat poison recently?'" Damien chuckled. But when he looked at Barry, his eyes seemed full.

"Aeey, man, you OK? What's going on? You've been acting all strange ever since we left the hospital. Don't tell me you and Amy are having problems." Damien looked at his younger brother.

"Whatever you do, man, don't follow in my footsteps. My life is pretty fucked up right now," Damien advised. Barry's eyebrows inched upward.

"You know what I mean," Damien said. "Besides, things will be different for you and Amy. I have a feeling."

"I wish you were right about that. But honestly, there may not even be an Amy and me!"

"What!" Damien could hardly believe his ears. "What the hell happened?"

"Quit playing hard to get, and let's go back to the bedroom. Need I remind you, we have some unfinished business to handle? Remember, last time we was here you went running out after only a few hours. Kinda left me hanging," Reginald said to Candy.

He hoped she knew what he wanted. He needed her to work her magic more than ever before. Reginald figured she was probably wondering what kind of tip she'd walk away with. Lucky for her, he was in a very generous mood.

Candy took off the clothes she had been lounging in.

"I see you're in page thirteen from the fall issue of Frederick's of Hollywood's catalog. Nice choice," Reginald said, unbuckling his pants.

Candy strutted over to the sofa. In one fluid movement, she leaned over the thick arm of the couch.

"Damn, like that?" Reginald moved closer, inspecting her as he zeroed in. He licked his lips in anticipation.

"Ah, wait, Pappy. You going raw?" she asked, looking back at him.

Reginald stood stroking his massive, stiff erection. He couldn't tear his eyes off Candy's pink flesh. Her opening was all but calling out to him. He swore he could see it throbbing, moving in and out with the walls contracting right before his eyes.

"Yeah, I'm gonna need to just put it in for a little while. I just wanna feel you, baby! That's all," he said. Candy hesitated a little bit at first. She braced herself against the sofa's arm.

"OK, but just remember that's gonna cost you extra. You OK with that?"

Reginald slapped her on the ass and pulled her garter belt so that it smacked against her skin.

"Ssssss." She giggled.

Without any further delay, Reginald jammed his member into her and began stroking with maximum strength and power.

He finally felt important, finally felt in charge, more importantly, he felt at home.

* * *

Barry wanted to run from the room, run from his brother's questions, but he knew that wouldn't help. First he rubbed his face, sighed, then shook his head.

When the phone rang again, he looked toward it with wide-eyed fear.

"You want me to get it?" Damien asked. Barry looked as if the phone was possessed.

"Nnn-no, just let the machine get it," he said.

"Man, who keeps calling here anyway? You think I don't notice when the phone rings you get all scared and worked up? You don't owe anybody money, do you?"

Barry looked up at his brother. If only he knew. It seemed an eternity passed before Barry summoned up the courage to confide in Damien. He released a heavy sigh.

"Well, I'm in trouble," he calmly stated. Barry felt so helpless as he uttered those words. He was in trouble, and he couldn't see a way out.

The phone rang again.

This time, Damien got up and snatched the receiver.

"Hello!" he all but screamed into the phone. Barry watched as his brother stood near the kitchen counter.

"You the one keep calling here every five minutes?"

Damien shook his head as if the caller could see him.

"Yeah, this Damien. Nah, I don't know nothing about you. W-what?" He turned to Barry. When his brows creased, Barry didn't have to wonder what the hell Sissy was saying.

"Oh, really?" Damien said. "Well, look, I need to talk to my brother, so I suggest you stop calling and wait for him to call you. Uh huh," Damien said.

"Well, since you know we're here, why do you keep calling? That must mean he's busy or he don't want to talk to you!" Damien walked back to the couch with the phone. "Look, I'm not about to argue with you, Sissy. Actually, I'm about to hang up, 'cause this ain't getting us nowhere. I'll tell Barry to call you. If he wants to, he will. If not, he won't. It's just that simple."

Barry noticed Damien frowning again.

"What the hell did you say? Who you threatening? You don't know me. I'm not my baby brother!" Damien screamed.

When he couldn't take it anymore, Barry got up and snatched the phone cord from the wall.

"I guess that's your trouble, huh?" Damien asked the minute he realized the line went dead.

"Um, yeah. That's sort of my fiancée," Barry admitted quietly.

"What?" Damien looked at the phone. "Isn't Amy your fiancée?"

Barry nodded and lowered his head. "It's all a huge mess. I don't know how I got myself into this. She wrote this letter telling me that she has a tape of Amy and me, and she's threatening to expose us if I don't go through with her plans," Barry admitted.

"Wait a minute. What's on the tape?" Damien wanted to know.

When Barry burst into tears, and could barely speak, Damien walked over and patted him on the back.

"Damn, okay. Look, we'll talk about it later, but I

just don't understand. Why would you propose to this crazy freak?"

"That's what you don't get. I didn't. She went out and bought her own engagement ring, then she proposed. According to one of the ten thousand messages she left today alone, she's already planned the wedding too. She told me I needed to check with the Gee-man about when he can marry us."

At first Damien didn't say anything. Then suddenly he busted out laughing hysterically.

Barry felt dejected. He couldn't find an ounce of humor in his situation.

CHAPTER 12

Sweetwater Powerhouse of God's members were starting to lose their patience. Rumors were circulating about their great leader, and answers were nowhere to be found. Then there was the stream of guest pastors. On Wednesdays and Sundays, Pastor Goodlove sat as an observer instead of performing his electrifying sermons from the pulpit.

Mama Sadie and the rest of the church elders, including the deacons and ushers, had called an emergency meeting. Deacon Martin had the floor. He looked back at the group with narrowing eyes.

"So what's it gonna be? I don't have to tell you all what this foolishness is doing to the fabric of our beloved church. Sweetwater is supposed to be the ultimate shelter in midst of the storm. But lately it's been a bed of festering scandal, and a melting pot for sinful behavior." Mama Sadie jumped up from her chair.

"Look, we need you to get to the point. I mean, what are you trying to say?"

"Yeah," Geraldine added.

"I mean, you just sitting up here repeating stuff we already know. Do you have a suggestion? A plan? Or you just wanted to take the floor to practice your preaching, 'cause baby we already know everything you talking 'bout. We here to take some action!"

"Praise the Lord," one of the holy rollers added. Deacon Martin looked around the room.

"Um, well, all I'm trying to say is things are changing around here, and we need to do something about it."

Mama Sadie walked up to center stage.

"OK, we got some decisions to make. You all know don't nobody love Pastor Goodlove the way I do. I love me some Pastor Goodlove. I have been here from the beginning when his daddy, rest his soul, founded Sweetwater. But I have long said things wasn't right in the Lord's house, and now we have allowed them to get way outta hand." She walked to the other side of the room. "I know nobody wants to think bad things—sinful, shameful things—about their beloved pastor. But I say something has got to be done. Let's look at the facts."

Ms. Geraldine passed Mama Sadie a folder. She opened it and started to flip through the pages.

"Before our beloved first lady, the late Carol Goodlove, was warm in her grave, the pastor was already out searching for her replacement." Mama Sadie made eye contact with a few of the members before she continued.

"We all know the jezebel he waltzed up in here with. She ain't even an active member of the Women's Auxiliary. Then there's the issue of her inappropriate clothing. How many times have we asked the pastor to speak to her, or do something about it, and still, nothing," she sighed dramatically.

"She's just a heathen," someone interjected.

"Then there were the stories about the three Goodlove boys. We have watched those boys grow into men right before our very eyes. How many of you in here babysat them chilren?" Mama Sadie scanned the room for the number of hands that flew into the air.

"I'm sure some of you, like me, with the exception of Barry, the youngest, are asking yourselves, where did we go wrong? That oldest, Damien, runs through the very young women of this church like he's Lucifer himself. The way he chases the flesh, one wouldn't think he was raised in a God-fearing home. And he's married!"

"Emph, Emph, Emph!" someone chimed in.

"Then that middle one, always looking at his daddy with evil in his eyes. Just the other day he walked right by me without as much as uttering a hello!" Mama Sadie shook her head.

"And then there's the issue that brought us all to this emergency meeting, taking time away from our most precious ministry work." Mama Sadie closed her eyes and sighed.

"Be strong," one of the holy rollers encouraged.

Mama Sadie swallowed back tears. She pulled a handkerchief from her bosom and dabbed at the corners of her eyes.

"To have such vile accusations circulating about our beloved pastor. I lose sleep at night thinking about all that is going on here at Sweetwater."

Mama Sadie looked back at the group. She had regained some of her composure.

"I say it's time to take these matters to the board. We're not just talking about an abomination of all that is holy . . . homosexuality? But let's look at the church affairs. We've heard nothing more on the expansion. The bank ledgers each elder, deacon, usher, and board member used to get stopped coming years ago. And when you ask that middle one, the accountant, he looks at you like you're speaking gibberish."

Mama Sadie paused again, then continued.

"I think we have no choice but to take these matters to the board," she announced again.

Michelle, Kim, and Tammy were in the church parking lot. They had just endured yet another guest pastor who nearly put the entire congregation to sleep. For the first time in the church's history, it appeared attendance was actually down. There were tons of empty seats in Wednesday night's Bible study. The three women had slipped out early.

"What is going on around here?" Tammy asked.

"We haven't seen Pastor Goodlove in days. We can't get answers about anything. The luncheon was cancelled. And who is picking these guest pastors?" Kim chimed in. Michelle looked around.

"Oh, shoot. I left my purse in there. Come back with me?" Tammy looked at Kim.

"I'm not going back in there," she said.

"Then I guess I'm not going to dinner with you guys," Michelle threatened.

"Hmmm, OK." Tammy gave in. "But I'm not staying long. We'll wait outside the door. You go in, grab your purse, and come right back out!"

They had just barely made it into the building

when two officers followed behind them. Kim and Tammy stayed in the hall when Michelle walked into the classroom behind the two officers. The guest pastor stopped speaking and everyone looked toward the officers. An usher quickly rushed toward the officers.

"Yes?" One of the officers looked around.

"We're looking for a Jazzlyn Cooper," he whispered.

Michelle stopped what she was doing and turned her attention to the usher talking to the officers. She grabbed her purse and walked directly toward the three of them.

"Ah, Mary, let me see if I can help these officers. We don't need to disrupt Bible study." The officers looked at her.

"And you are?"

"Oh, my father-in-law is the pastor here, the Reverend Ethan Goodlove III. Can we take this outside?"

The usher went back to her chair and allowed Michelle to guide the officer outside.

Outside, Tammy and Kim didn't even try to act like they weren't eavesdropping.

"Officers, may I ask what this is about?"

"We're looking for Ms. Cooper. We were told Bible study started at six."

"It does, but she's not here. She doesn't typically come to Bible study. If you'd like, I could get a current address and phone number for her," Michelle offered.

"No need. We've been by her place. When do you expect to see her again?"

"Ah, she'll be here Sunday morning. I'm not sure if this matter can wait that long. I could tell her to call you," Michelle said.

"No need. If we have to, we'll come back. Thanks for your time, Mrs. Goodlove."

CHAPTER 13

The guest pastor just couldn't seem to work his jelly the way Pastor Goodlove did. Out of courtesy, a few members did the expected "Praise the Lord," and there were a few "Amen, pastors," and even a couple of "hallelujahs." But nothing he did even slightly held a candle to Pastor Goodlove.

He was missing and sorely missed. Mama Sadie didn't even catch the spirit. That's when most people realized there really was trouble at Sweetwater.

For weeks, the rumors had been swirling. At first, little whispers here and there, but in the past few days, the rumors had picked up momentum. Now it was all that most members thought about when they came to church.

For his part, Pastor Goodlove was keeping a low profile. Reginald had gone out and hired an attorney, the best in Houston, but things still weren't the same.

Pastor Goodlove sat on his throne and looked out approvingly. Occasionally, he'd nod when the pastor said something. He showed a few smiles, but he never got up to personally address the church.

Theola sat in the first pew. She struggled to remain awake. All she needed was to fall asleep and get Mama Sadie and the holy rollers on her case. She didn't understand who was responsible for inviting Pastor Smith. At the end of his sermon, he looked toward the congregation.

"I was thrilled to be here for you today. But before we go, some of the church elders want to make a special presentation."

Ms. Geraldine got up and walked to the microphone next to the pulpit. Two of the other holy rollers got up and shuffled to the back of the church. Mama Sadie tossed a dirty look over at Theola and glanced disapprovingly at her raunchy outfit. Theola rolled her eyes.

"Giving all praises to the almighty Lord and Savior Jesus Christ, all honors to Pastor Goodlove, and my brothers and sisters in Christ." Ms. Geraldine smiled and unfolded a piece of paper.

"As most of you may know, the annual Purple Tea Luncheon is right around the corner. For reasons I need not mention, ticket sales have been the lowest in Sweetwater's history." She glanced over at Theola. "Some of us have respectfully declined an invitation to the luncheon, but wanted to have our event which pays homage to the original First Lady to be recognized on the same level."

Before she finished her speech, two of the other holy rollers struggled to drag a large, gold easel with a covered frame to the middle of the sanctuary.

Ms. Geraldine stopped talking as if they needed quiet to complete their mission.

"On behalf of the original founding members of the Sweetwater Powerhouse of God's Women's Auxiliary, we want to unveil a portrait of Sweetwater's first lady. A few people started clapping their hands.

Theola gasped and covered her mouth. When had the tide changed? And how come no one even mentioned anything to her? She actually felt bad about them not telling the holy rollers the luncheon had been cancelled. Theola reached for her clutch purse and dug deep for tissue. She couldn't believe these people were about to make her cry. *It's about time that they acknowledged me*, she thought.

Once the easel was in place, the two ladies reclaimed their seats. In a very dramatic move, Mama Sadie, who had dressed for the occasion in a glittering purple suit, walked up, and stood next to the covered easel. She nodded to Geraldine, who spoke on cue.

"So we hope that the pastor and you all will join us in lifting our first lady's spirit in hopes that she will watch over us at all times."

When the word "times" fell from her lips, Mama Sadie pulled the cover to reveal the smiling face of the late Mrs. Carol Goodlove.

The crowd's reaction varied. There were some gasps, a few chuckles, and lots of whispers. Soon, people sitting way in the back were standing up and stretching their necks to see what was going on up front.

In that instant, the color disappeared from Theola's face. She looked at the portrait, then at the holy rollers. Michelle looked at Theola like she wanted to cry for her.

Swallowing back tears, Theola grabbed her purse, her coat, and her Bible, and strolled down the aisle with her head held high. She walked out of the church and got into her car.

CHAPTER 14

"That was totally uncalled for. It was rude, disrespectful, and embarrassing. We had company for goodness' sake!" Pastor Goodlove had Mama Sadie and the rest of the holy rollers holed up in his office.

He had been dishing out a good tongue lashing for at least twenty minutes.

"What do you even have to say for yourselves?" he asked.

The women looked at each other.

"You guys are supposed to be the elders of this church. We're supposed to look toward you for guidance and help with these young up-and-comers."

The ladies remained silent.

A knock at his office door interrupted the one-sided conversation. Pastor Goodlove looked toward the door, and Geraldine jumped up to answer it.

Reginald stood there with two other men at his side.

"Mr. Watson, Mr. Tyler," she quickly said, "You need to meet with the pastor? Well, we were just leaving." At the sight of the lawyers who had become members of Sweetwater by default, the women quickly scurried out of the office.

When he thought his wife would be at work, Damien convinced his brother to take him by the house. He needed to get more clothes, and truthfully, he had started missing his place. Since he still wasn't sure who was behind the attempt on his life, he saw nothing wrong with the fact that he hadn't talked to his wife in nearly two weeks.

Damien gave his brother a cross look when he had to swerve the car to avoid the huge Salvation Army truck. It had pulled away from the curb in front of Damien's house.

"Man, I've never seen a truck that big before, not a Salvation Army one anyway," Damien said.

"Yeah, someone must've made a huge donation," Barry remarked as he let his brother out of the car.

When Damien unlocked the front door to his house, his heart suddenly dropped to his toes.

His knees buckled and he suddenly had to lean on the wall for support. As Damien glanced around the empty room, taking in the bare walls, he felt himself beginning to hyperventilate. He looked around the living room and saw absolutely nothing. The furniture, his electronics, Michelle's plants, the kids' toys—all of it was gone! Barry was parking the car and hadn't arrived inside yet.

"Oh, sweet Jesus!" Damien mumbled. He used his hands to slap his head as his brother walked up to the door. Barry stepped inside and looked around.

"What happened here? You guys moving or something?"

Damien couldn't find his voice. His mind could only think about all that was missing. There was no proof that he had lived in the house, that anyone had occupied it at all.

With his heart beating hard and fast, he anxiously ran to the back where the bedrooms and family rooms were. When he arrived, there it was: a drastic repeat of what had slapped him in the face when he first stepped into the house he once called home.

Everything was gone. The carpets were noticeably clean, as if they'd recently been shampooed and steamed. The tile sparkled on the kitchen floor. Crayon marks his children made on the walls were gone, and the entire place reeked of fresh paint. The window treatments, custom drapes, and kitchen curtains were gone too. The wooden blinds had been wiped clean. Even the countertops glistened. All of the appliances had a shine that could've passed for new. Damien looked around in utter and absolute disbelief. He was in distress.

When he turned around, his brother was standing behind him, taking in the empty house.

"Does this mean Michelle left you?" Barry asked.

Damien ran to their master bedroom. Before he made it up the stairs, he already knew just what to expect. But still he held out hope. Damien took a deep breath and even closed his eyes before clutching the doorknob. Caressing the cold, hard knob, he finally mustered up the courage to turn it and step inside.

Their expensive cherry wood bedroom suite, the antique writing table that housed his great, great grandfather's Bible, the towels in the grand master bathroom, his clothes, even his shoes—all of it was gone.

"Oh my God!" he shrieked.

Barry rushed upstairs to find Damien lying in the middle of the bedroom floor. Damien cried, hard and loud. He held his head, balled himself into a fetal position, and cried.

Reginald still couldn't believe he had spent so much money on sex. Every time he got his phone bill or the other one that came in the plain, brown envelope, he suffered sticker shock.

"Damn, the entire twenty-five grand, gone, just like that, in a matter of days." He shook his head in disbelief.

But the memories, oh, he'd cherish the memories of the wicked but pleasurable things Candy did to his body. She had been worth every dime of his money. Well, it wasn't quite his money, but hell, as hard as he worked for it, it may as well be his. And he spent it on whatever his heart desired. Reginald lived modestly, but spent like a high roller every time Candy was on his arm.

As he walked around his small efficiency, he wished for even more money. Lately he'd been daydreaming about what life would be like if he, instead of the Gee man, owned the purse strings.

Reginald found himself often thinking about life after the Gee man. He wondered how much of his fortune Gee would leave to them. He sighed.

"Knowing that old, greedy bastard, he'd probably try to get the money buried with him," he said.

Reginald walked to the small refrigerator and opened the door.

He looked at the bottle of outdated milk, the small carton of eggs, and something wrapped in foil. The freezer looked even worse. There he had two half empty ice trays, a half empty bag of okra, and a Hungry Man TV dinner. Trouble was, he didn't know how long the TV dinner had been there.

When he picked it up and saw an expiration date of January 1999, he tossed it back into the freezer.

"Damn, that's nearly six years old," he hissed.

He gave up on finding food and went to the living room. Reginald sat on his La-Z-Boy recliner, the only thing to sit on in the room, and turned on the TV. It was a fourteen-inch black and white that sat on a milk crate.

"Maybe I should call and see what Candy is doing," he said. He shook his head. "Nah, that bitch already got enough of my money."

He reclined his chair and yawned. There was nothing worth watching on TV. If he had cable, he might've been able to pull up a good game, but he didn't have money to waste on such a luxury.

After reclining for a few minutes, Reginald grabbed the phone book and telephone. He flipped through to the escort section and decided at that moment to find himself a new date. Once everything was set up, he walked over to his bed and kneeled down on the floor.

He dug out the extra checkbook and wrote himself a check for fifty thousand dollars. He felt an instant rush the moment he forged the necessary signatures.

* * *

As Barry watched his brother bawling on the floor, he didn't miss the irony of the situation. He wasn't thinking about Damien finally getting what he deserved for years of running around on his wife. Instead, he thought about how in his own moment of darkness, this was the man he wanted to turn to for help.

A sudden feeling of helplessness came over him. When Damien had hung up on Sissy, Barry finally thought he might have a chance.

But seeing Damien now, and how he was basically unable to handle his own problems, Barry knew for sure he'd have to deal with Sissy on his own.

When he finally grew tired of watching his big brother cry like a helpless baby, he stooped down and reached out to him.

"Come on, Dee, let's get out of here," Barry said.

"I can't believe this. Where are my girls? She took my kids from me, she took all my stuff," Damien wailed.

Barry patted him on his back because he didn't know what else to say or do.

"Man, let's go," Barry said.

Damien finally rolled onto his back. He used his forearm to cover his eyes. His cries had subsided a bit, but he was still heaving.

"Why don't we go somewhere to get your mind off of this?" Barry offered.

Damien was sniffling by now. He sat upright and looked around the empty room. He rubbed his eyes, and then looked up at his baby brother.

"Guess I really fucked up this time, huh?"

Barry didn't know what to say to that. It was very

obvious that Damien had messed up, but Barry didn't think he needed to remind him. Looking around the room again, Damien shook his head.

"Man, this is really deep, but sitting here ain't gonna bring her or your kids back," Barry said.

Damien didn't respond right away. Soon he stuck his hand out to his brother. Barry helped pull him up from the floor and they both walked back outside to the car.

When they pulled up to a stoplight, they looked confused as they both jerked forward.

BAM!

"What the fuck?" Damien hollered as he looked out the back window. "I know somebody didn't just rear-end us," he said.

Barry tried to pull his car over to the right side of the road. But before he could maneuver the vehicle off the road, it happened again.

BAM!

"Shit!" Damien said.

This time Barry turned around to see what was going on. An accident maybe once, but certainly not twice.

What the hell, he thought. When he looked over his shoulder and saw Sissy behind the wheel of a Hummer, he punched his pedal and sped off.

"Shit! Who is that?" Damien asked, looking over his own shoulder.

"That was Sissy," Barry said as he sped away from her.

"Oh hell, nah. That bitch is crazy!"

"What do you think I've been trying to warn you about?" Barry said.

CHAPTER 15

The Sunday sermons at Sweetwater PG had taken a drastic turn for the worse. For the first time in the church's history, empty chairs were scattered all throughout the sanctuary. And it was quite noticeable. Most Sundays, one would be hard-pressed to find an empty chair even in the overflow room, much less enough of them to count.

Pastor Goodlove himself was daydreaming as he listened to the tired and outdated sermon from Pastor Safford. He didn't understand how these men expected success when they refused to change with the times. They were still delivering the message in that old fashioned gibberish that did nothing to inspire parishioners.

He also knew that most of the Sweetwater members who were present were only trying to show their loyalty. Although Pastor Goodlove was not delivering the sermon, he did plan to address the congregation about a very important issue.

After a brief meeting with Reginald before service, he was warned that a downward trend was starting to take shape, and he needed to do something about it quickly. Pastor Goodlove didn't love anything more than his money, so he decided to take his son's advice. They were already trying to implement new ways in which to separate members from their hard earned money. He had asked Reginald to look into a direct deposit system, similar to what they did with income tax returns. The plan involved having a handful of members agreeing to have their paychecks deposited directly into the church's account, then the church would pay their bills and help them better handle their finances.

Pastor remembered the look on his son's face when he discussed details of the plan. Reginald looked as if he had swallowed something sour.

"Who in the world would go for something like that?" he had asked.

"Members of Sweetwater are very trustworthy. They know their pastor knows what's best for them."

"But you're talking about taking over people's finances!"

"I'm talking about fostering a better relationship among the members and the church son. If we teach members how to handle their finances, their lives would be free of stress and worry. You've got to look at the bigger picture." Pastor Goodlove shook his head. He wondered why he was even explaining anything to Reginald.

"Just look into it," he snapped, closing the conversation for good.

Pastor Goodlove wanted someone to come and put Pastor Safford out of his misery, and bring an end to everyone else's. That thought brought him back to the dire situation at hand.

When he figured the guest pastor was done, he jumped up from his throne. He really did jump, and it was right on time because he felt himself nodding off.

"Ah, before we go to prayer," Pastor Goodlove said as he walked toward the pulpit then away from it, "there are a few things we need to talk about."

"Amen! Pastor!" someone yelled from the back.

"Now, that's what I'm talking about," another voice mumbled.

Parishioners started sitting upright in their seats. Some became more alert and acted like they were more focused. They were ready for some of Pastor's electrifying words.

"Sweetwater is going through a rough patch," the pastor said. He looked around the church before continuing. "You see, for years this sanctuary has been just that, a sanctuary, a cover from the storm, shelter during the turbulent storm." He held up a finger. "You see, many of you have turned to Sweetwater for healing, for help, and understanding. But now, it seems that at least some, not all, but some of you are forgetting those times."

Pastor Goodlove paused and shook his head. He tisked.

"I'll bet it would surprise many of you to know that some of your own Sweetwater family members are slipping on the job."

There were a few gasps. It was what he'd hoped for.

"You see, a church is a building. It's the members and their dedication that make it strong. And when you fall down on your financial obligations, it's like saying you don't care about your sanctuary. I've been advised that 20 percent of you are not making good on your monthly installments. Twenty percent!" Pastor Goodlove shook his head as if he was really disappointed with the figure. He tried to make eye contact with a few members. "Now you remember what that commitment was all about, right?" Pastor Goodlove looked around the church.

He saw many heads hanging.

"You have committed to eight to twenty-five hundred dollars a month. Now I don't want to start calling names, but if you don't pay what you committed to, well, you're gonna force me to say some thangs. And we all know how church folk can be. Oh, we may be Christians, but we can talk about folk." Pastor Goodlove chuckled, and then waved them off as he slipped into his chambers.

The two officers walked in right as the members finished tithing. One of the ushers in the back met them near the back door.

Soon the ushers and the officers were scanning the room.

By the time Theola noticed the officers, she knew something was wrong. They weren't the uniformed officers who worked as security guards or helped park cars. These two officers were new.

She saw them speak with an usher, then start looking around the congregation. Theola leaned toward the back as she noticed the officers approach Jazzlyn.

Although she wasn't close enough to hear what was being said, she didn't need to be. The accusations rippled all up to the front pews.

"She's being charged with administering poison with intent to kill," someone said.

Damn, arrested in church, Theola thought. Despite this, she was willing to bet some of Sweetwater's members would rather wrap their arms around someone like Jazzlyn before they'd spit on Theola if she were on fire. Theola had no idea why people in the church despised her so. She couldn't get over the fact that these were so-called Christians, born-again Christians at that, and just plain ole people who were supposed to know better.

They talked about her constantly, gossiped about things they thought she was doing, and most of them didn't even have the decency to speak to her. If they weren't talking about her clothes, it was what she was driving. And when it wasn't that, it was the color of her fingernails. When they grew tired of that, they focused in on her makeup. And that's while they were in the house of the Lord!

She was really getting tired of their foolishness. If this was really what true Christians behaved like, she'd rather remain a heathen. That, among other things, is what they called her.

It was sad for her to admit it, but spite was what made her keep going to church despite the abuse. Every time she thought about staying away, she realized that if she did that, she might make the gossipers think they had accomplished their goal.

Theola wanted them to know she had been through far worse than anything they could call her, or say about her. She was orphaned at the age of three, bounced from foster home to foster home, and had still made something of herself as far as she was concerned. She could've been stuck in the projects with a houseful of kids; instead, she was living like royalty. It wasn't her fault she lucked up on a good thing, and she wasn't ashamed of it either. She wore the best labels money could buy, lived in a sprawling mansion, and had her choice of expensive vehicles to drive.

She lived better with Ethan than she ever had in her entire life. But she was becoming tired of the foolishness at church. She was also tired of the rumors floating around about his sexuality. She didn't want to give into that stuff, but she was sick of having to beg the old man for sex. She knew he took Viagra, but she didn't care.

When he got up and gave that line about people not paying their monthly dues, she just considered it more money for her to spend. The minute her husband disappeared into his chambers, she got up and walked out the back door.

Sometimes she didn't care if she ever saw the inside of Sweetwater PG and its members again.

CHAPTER 16

"**O**HMIGOD!" Damien gasped when he arrived in his brother's driveway. His car was sitting on flattened tires. All four of the tires had been slashed. Someone had carved lewd comments into the paint with a key, and the tomatoes and eggs they used to stain the windows now stained both the car and the concrete.

Damien was about to walk back into the house and just pretend like he never stepped outside in the first place. He still hadn't talked to Michelle or his children. He'd spent so much time calling; he thought he'd get arthritis in his fingers from dialing. But regardless of how many times he called, he got Michelle's voicemail.

He knew she was staying at her parents' house, but he wasn't brave enough to go there. He had no idea what she had told them. Damien told himself that regardless of what happened between him and Michelle, she'd better not try to keep his kids away from him. But that's exactly what was happening. And there was nothing he could do about it.

Instead of going back into the house, Damien dug into his pockets and pulled out his cell phone. After the operator connected him to the Fort Bend County Sheriff's Department, he explained that a crime had been committed against his property, and he needed to know his options. The sheriff's department said they would send someone out to the house to take a report. He wondered just how long that would take, but decided he'd just have to wait it out. He and Barry were planning on running out, but that too would have to wait.

The female officer shook her head after she snapped the last picture of Damien's car.

"Any idea who might want to deliberately do something like this to you? We haven't had any similar reports of vandalism in this neighborhood," she said.

Damien wanted so badly to implicate Jazzlyn, but the truth was, he couldn't. He kept thinking there was no way Jazzlyn could carry this out alone.

"Sir?" the officer asked with feigned annoyance.

"Well, not really," Damien confessed.

The officer's brow inched upward. She pursed her lips, immediately stopped writing, and put one hand on her hip.

"Mr. Goodlove, what is this really about?" she asked.

The last thing Damien wanted to do was explain the whole torrid story. But he couldn't help feeling like Jazzlyn was somehow involved, so he started at the beginning and laid it all out.

"You stupid ass, hoish bastard! You got the fucking audacity to pick up the phone and call me after what you did!" Jazzlyn's voice screamed through the phone.

"What are you talking about? What did I ever do to you, Jazz?" Damien asked.

"Oh, so now you stuck on stupid, right?"

"What are you talking about? I didn't do anything to deserve this. You fucked up my car. That just wasn't right!"

"Oh, you deserved that and then some. You just don't know the trouble you've gotten me into, and what am I supposed to do? I'm all by myself. I ain't got no husband to take care of me!" Damien rubbed his temple; a migraine was threatening to push through. He and Barry were supposed to be heading over to see the Gee man. He didn't have time to listen to her senseless rambling.

"I'm missing something here. I didn't do anything to you!" he said. "You're mad about Gina?" he finally asked, giving up.

"At this point I don't even care who you stick that thang of yours in. But you are gonna pay for what you did to me. You could've been a man about yours. You could've came and asked me. Instead, you took the punk way out. But that's OK, though."

"Girl, what are you talking about?" Damien gave up.

"Oh, don't even act like you didn't know what was gonna happen in church. That's why your punk ass didn't show up! I don't even know what I saw in you!"

"Jazzlyn? Why are you tripping? I don't know what you're talking about. No, I wasn't in church, but what's that got to do with you?"

Damien moved the phone from his ear when she laughed sarcastically.

"Like you don't know . . . or should I say like you didn't know the police came and arrested me! Yep, right there inside your precious Sweetwater PG! Right there for everyone to see, and point, and whisper, and chuckle. I can't stand your ass!"

"What? You were arrested?" Damien screamed. "What's that got to do with me?" Jazzlyn sucked her teeth, and then snickered.

"You tryin' ta tell me you didn't tell the police that I tried to kill you with rat poison? Oh, you are truly tired!" she screamed before hanging up the phone.

Reginald went by his father's office just to see what was going on. He wanted to know if the old man was the least bit suspicious.

But the minute Reginald walked in, Pastor Goodlove had a scowl across his face that looked like he smelled something foul.

"Where the hell have you been?" he growled.

"What are you talking about? What's wrong?" Reginald tried to remain calm.

"You wanna know what's wrong? Have you been watching the damn news by any chance? If you had, you'd already know what's wrong. What the hell am I paying you for?"

Reginald looked to the floor. He should've followed his first instincts and went shopping after he cashed that check.

He didn't need this mess.

"Some reporter has been lurking around here asking questions about these accusations. You do remember the accusations, right? The same one you and your team of expensive lawyers are supposed to make go away!" Reginald shrugged.

"OK, so what happened? I mean, some reporter comes asking questions." Reginald shrugged easily. "That's never bothered you before. You didn't do anything wrong, remember? So, who really cares if some sleezy reporter is asking questions? Let 'em ask."

Before Reginald knew what was happening, his father had him by the lapels and was in his face. He felt the old man's breath, smelled it. As he screamed, his saliva assaulted Reginald's face.

"Boy, who the hell are you talking to like that? I pay you good money so I don't have to worry about that kind of madness. Then I gotta be calling all around town searching for your stupid ass!" Pastor Goodlove let him go. "Now act like you are grateful for the blessing I've given you and tell me where we are with this expansion." The pastor stood near his entertainment console.

Reginald swallowed back tears. He tried to pull himself together, but he couldn't. When his father spun around on his heels, Reginald actually felt himself tremble.

"Um, I wanted to tell you that the expansion—it's going well. I have to go back there next week," he said.

"Is that the best you can do?" Pastor Goodlove looked at him and he looked away. Reginald didn't want to be scrutinized anymore. He was sick and tired of being abused by his father.

He hadn't given the expansion another thought, and he was getting to the point where he could care less if they ever took their mission on the road again. Reginald thought about the fact that Pastor Goodlove's Beaumont campus was now suffering from his neglect.

Reginald wanted to talk to the Gee man about how this scandal was going to start impacting the bottom line. For the first time since a hurricane-mandated evacuation, the amount of money coming in through tithes and offerings had actually gone down. Wednesday night's love offering to the Pastor had also gone down slightly. Even the ATM machines placed throughout the building weren't being used as frequently. That meant the church wasn't getting its cut of the fees members were charged for the privilege of easy access to their own funds.

But Reginald couldn't bring himself to think about anything other than how he'd spend that fifty grand.

Sissy looked down the hall in both directions. When she didn't see anyone coming, she quickly slid the key into the lock and eased into Barry's condo. The last thing she needed was Damien's nosey ass sneaking around. She didn't want to have to curse him out again. Each time she tried to call her fiancé, Damien either hung up on her or just never gave the phone to Barry. She couldn't wait until he took his whoreish ass back home. It was like he was Barry's personal phone call screener.

She was tired of it, and was determined to put an end to the complete disrespect she was enduring. Sissy had even tried leaving messages for Barry, appealing to his heart by talking about their pending wedding, but it never worked.

Lately she spent most of her time following Barry and Damien around. It looked like Barry's life had turned into doing everything for his brother. She was tired of that too. She needed Damien to pull himself together so that she and Barry could get back on track.

Once inside, Sissy went to work quickly. She checked for the miniature cameras and recording devices she had placed all over his apartment. She'd review them once she arrived back at her place. That was how she had stumbled on the little love tape of Barry and Amy. Her snooping skills had paid off in a huge way. She knew that prude would die if she ever knew that Sissy was in on their little secret. But it wasn't until after spending time with Barry and seeing him inter-acting with other church members that she realized just how valuable that tape really was.

Sissy decided to use the tape as her security blan-ket, just in case Barry thought he'd leave her for that little Ms. Goody-Two-Shoes, Amy. She was glad she had the tape.

Leaving was always the hardest part. Unlike when she arrived, she couldn't check the halls for Damien or Barry. When leaving, she had no way of knowing if they were lurking around or on their way in.

Sissy made it to the elevator without detection, only to have the doors open to Barry's smiling face.

It was a smile that vanished the minute his eyes ze-roed in on her.

"This must be my lucky day," she sang. Sissy smiled and stuck her chest out. "Hi, Barry. I was just looking for you." She looked at Damien, who didn't have the normal smug look on his face. He looked like he'd been crying.

"Aeey, dog—I mean Damien," Sissy said.

"What are you doing here?" Barry asked. When she didn't respond, he lightly pushed past her and walked into the hall. "I don't have time for this, not right now," he warned. She was surprised Damien didn't call her out of her name. Lately those two had been going at it something fierce.

"Well, I need to talk to you . . . and it's personal," she said, eyeing Damien. "You think we could talk for a few minutes, you know, in private?"

Barry looked like he wanted to say no. But much to her surprise, he actually stopped walking and gave his key to Damien. Sissy was glad she wasn't caught inside his condo. She had borrowed her coworker's car, and parked on the opposite side of his building, but still, she had a feeling nothing good would come from her constant close encounters with being caught.

"You should tell your brother to respect his future sister-in-law," Sissy said. When she felt herself losing his attention, she quickly changed the topic. "I came here because I wanted to talk to you about where you are with Amy. I'm so ready for us to move on. Also, we should register together. I did Foley's and Bed Bath & Beyond, but I thought you'd want to be there when I did Crate and Barrel."

"I'm not marrying you," Barry said straight-forwardly.

Sissy felt her stomach churn.

"OK, wait, wait." She started flapping her arms. "You don't know what you're saying. Let's not get hasty. We can work this out. We were meant to be." She reached for his hands. Barry shook his head.

"You beg me to marry you, buy your own damn ring, and now you want to talk about us being meant to be?" He shrugged. "Let's get real."

Sissy looked at Barry and rolled her eyes before relying on the wall for strength. She knew he only said those things to hurt her feelings, but she had worked too hard to turn back now.

She shook her head at the things he said. She hadn't begged Barry to marry her. And yes, she bought the ring, but once she became his wife, she'd earn that money back ten times over. He was, after all, son of the very talented and very rich Ethan Goodlove III.

Sissy was pissed. This had to be Damien's influence rearing its ugly head. She still had to get home and review the tapes, but now she didn't know what she was going to do.

"You need to get over it. I don't care what you do with that tape. I'm not marrying you no matter what you got against me. You can tell anybody you want. Hell, why don't you set up a private screening at the church? I don't care anymore. Do what you gotta do, because I'm marrying Amy, not you!" he spat before turning and walking away.

"You'll be sorry," she cried to his back. "You'll be sorry, Barry Goodlove. I swear you'll be sorry!"

Inside, Damien looked at his brother.

"You tell her, man?"

"Yeah," he said.

"What did she say or do?"

"You don't hear her screaming out there?" Damien stopped talking.

"Dang, what you do to that girl? You know what, if she doesn't leave in a few minutes, we need to call the police."

"OK, cool," Barry said.

CHAPTER 17

As Pastor Watson rambled on about the true meaning of a Biblical phrase, Pastor Goodlove started thinking about the state of his beloved Sweetwater.

Attendance was down, folks were gossiping, and for the first time in a long while, he had to start thinking about ways to bring the finances up again.

Even after he made his appeal for members to stay true to their financial commitment, records continued to show that not too many people were following his warning.

As he sat listening to the guest pastor's poor excuse for a sermon, his mind lingered on the interview he saw on TV the night before. He wondered if he should address the church. He knew his congregation had questions. Hell, he had even heard some of the misinformation floating around. And he wasn't sure if he agreed with the attorneys that silence was the best way to handle these matters.

As the pastor looked out into the crowd, he knew that some of his parishioners would always remain loyal, and he was happy about that.

* * *

Michelle hadn't missed a day of church since she moved out. Her parents thought she was crazy to return to Sweetwater. They had already switched their memberships and their granddaughters' memberships to Sugar Hollow Missionary Baptist Church.

"Baby, there's just too much going on in that church for us to stay. And the mess goes from the pastor on down," her mother had said.

But Michelle refused to budge. She continued to go to Sweetwater, thinking she might eventually run into her husband, but so far she hadn't. Since Jazzlyn's arrest, she hadn't seen her either. For all she knew, the two dogs were probably together, getting all worked up and screwing in some alley.

She also couldn't stop thinking about the many pictures and videos her husband had in his secret hiding place in their house.

Michelle was just disgusted when she found a set of pictures with other women in her lingerie! The thought brought tears to her eyes.

"What the hell?" she had said. She opened the box and pulled out the pictures. When she looked closer at the skank, she had to do a double take. "Is this my lace halter teddy?" She held the picture closer. "Nah, who'd be nasty enough to wear another woman's lingerie?" Michelle held the picture closer to the light. She put it to the side and flipped through the rest.

There were tons of pictures of women in sexually explicit poses. Another one caught her eye. The picture confirmed her worst fear. A healthy woman was squeezed into Michelle's fur trimmed white satin gown. It was long and sexy on Michelle, but on the woman it clearly dragged on the floor. She even had her crusty feet in the matching, fur-trimmed, high-heeled slippers. Michelle dropped the picture as if it had seared her fingertips.

"Oh my God! That's disgusting!" Not only had her husband allowed his mistresses to wear her lingerie, but then the fool took pictures of them in it. She shook her head.

When she ran her fingers across a videotape, she shuddered to even think about what she might see. Michelle had packed up all of his things for the Salvation Army donation and was just going through and trying to figure out what she'd toss and what she'd keep.

On the first of several videotapes, she saw her husband walk into their bedroom with another woman. Michelle began to sob. When Damien told the woman to look at what he had hand selected for her, Michelle got the confirmation she needed about whether he had other women wearing her lingerie and not just some exactly like it.

After she saw her husband riding one woman's large behind like she was an animal, and describing how much he enjoyed anal sex, she thought she'd be sick.

When Theola approached her after service, Michelle snapped out of those awful memories.

"Aeey, girl, how'er you holding up?" Theola asked. Michelle shook her head and sighed.

"I'm hanging in there the best I can, considering," she confirmed.

"Well, why don't you come out to Blueridge this afternoon? I could have the chef fix us something exotic to eat, then we could get drunk and talk about how stupid we were for fooling with these Goodlove men?" Theola shrugged.

Michelle couldn't believe Theola was wearing a tank top with a miniskirt and high-heeled boots. She thought about politely declining the offer, but then decided to accept.

"Yeah, I think I'll take you up on that. What time?"

Theola leaned in close. "Girl, let's go now. Leave your car here and I'll drive you."

Michelle shrugged. "Even better," she said.

CHAPTER 18

"So the question is, did you do anything to this young man that might have been taken the wrong way?"

Pastor Goodlove looked into the attorney's eyes. He didn't know how many ways he could ask the question. It had varied from "could your intentions have been misunderstood?" to "did you think you had permission to pursue this?"

"I don't know how many ways I can say this. I did not engage in sexual relations with that young man!" Pastor Goodlove was firm. "He came to me for spiritual guidance, he mentioned his current hardship, and I, on more than one occasion, wrote him a check."

"You can understand how eyebrows would be raised at the fact that you've given this young man nearly thirty-five thousand dollars, right?"

"Not at all." The attorney adjusted his body in his chair.

"Well, mister, ah, Pastor Goodlove, some might see that as hush money. Some could argue that you gave him this money because you wanted to buy his silence." Pastor Goodlove slapped his hands on his desk.

"I did nothing of the sort! I don't have to buy anyone's silence. I thought you all came here to address the concerns I had about approaching the congregation. I don't have time to keep repeating myself," he spat.

"Well, the truth is, the deposition is less than a month away, and we can't seem to get you to take this lawsuit seriously."

"I put my fate in the hands of the almighty God and no one else. That boy knows I did nothing but try to help him along his path with the Lord." The attorney shook his head.

"I don't think you understand." He reached into his satchel and pulled out a massive stack of papers.

Pastor Goodlove tried to hide his surprise, but he didn't do it well.

For the first time since the meeting began, he looked toward Reginald. But he didn't read concern on his son's face, so he swallowed and waited to hear what the attorney was about to say.

"I understand what you are saying. I really do." The attorney drummed his fingers across the stack of papers. "But what we've got is a serious problem brewing here. Since the two news stories about the drummer and his accusations, at least eleven other young men have come forward with different accusations."

Pastor Goodlove shrugged. "So, what's that got to do with me? And why are we here today?"

"Well, it's pretty simple really. While there will always be copycat cases, I have to tell you, some people will take a closer look at what these men are saying. Some people, like those who might get picked for a jury, if it ever went that far," the attorney said.

"Don't I pay you guys to take care of this stuff?" Pastor Goodlove huffed and looked at Reginald momentarily.

"The problem is, while most of these accusations may be false, a few of them are eerily similar enough, that a juror might easily be swayed." The attorney sat up. "That is, if it ever went that far. But it's our job to prepare you, just in case it does."

"Look, I just want to know what I can and cannot say to Sweetwater's members. They are well overdue when it comes to answers or just some information," Pastor Goodlove said.

"Well, what do you want to tell them?" the attorney asked.

"I was thinking about the truth," he answered.

The attorney shifted in his chair. "I'm not so sure that would be a good idea." He held his hand up and out toward Pastor Goodlove. "You pay for our expert advice. I urge you to take what you pay for. Yes, talk to your congregation, but be very careful about what you say. We don't want any of your words to come back and haunt you."

"It takes a whole lot to keep a good man down," Damien said to his reflection in the mirror. After he finished feeling sorry for himself, he again tried to reach his daughters at his in-laws' house. When he got the machine he'd grown accustom to leaving messages on, he decided to take life by the horns.

He picked up his Blackberry and scrolled through the secret list of names and numbers. This is where he stored the names of women he shared a special kinship with. He was going to lift his own spirits, the only way he knew how.

As he reviewed the names on his list, he dug into his leather bag and pulled open the secret compartment. There, he had a bunch of old panties and lingerie from women he deemed special.

Damien dialed Latangia Patterson's number. She left Sweetwater nearly a year ago, so he figured she'd be a safe bet.

"Aeey, girl," he said, the minute he heard her squeaky voice. Damien took a pair of pink, lacy thongs and sniffed them.

"I know this is not who I think it is," she squealed.

"It's me, baby. It's me." He smiled to himself. Yeah, he still had it. He balled the panties up in his hands, closed his eyes, then tried to remember the dozen or so behinds that had been lucky enough to grace the thongs.

"So when can we hook up?" she asked.

"See, that's why I like you, Latangia. You get straight to the point." Damien put the thongs back into his collection, then rubbed his crotch.

"I'm free tonight. What's up? You doing that family thing still?"

"Nah, baby, I'm free as a bird. I'm separated, so I figured I'd catch up with old friends and see what's going on. You know me," Damien said.

"Hmm, I sure do know you. So where you doing your dirt these days?" she asked.

"Oh, why I gotta be like that?"

"Damien Goodlove, we're cut from similar cloth,

so let's not fake it, baby. Our sex drives are always in overdrive. It's not a crime, but when you start lying to yourself, huh, something's wrong with that," she said.

"I feel you, girl," he said.

"No, not yet, but you can in about say three hours?"

"That'll work," he sang. "That'll work."

"OK, so you still hang out at the Magnolia Hotel?"

"Ain't been there since I was there with you," he said.

"Yeah, right! I'll meet you there at eight tonight!"

Damien was determined to make Michelle sorry she ever walked out on him. But before he even thought about seeing her, he was determined to have himself a little bit of fun living the single life.

He dug his hand deep into his collection and pulled out a red pair. They were small enough to be folded into the size of a silver dollar. Damien pulled the panties out and stretched them. He placed them over his face, laid back, closed his eyes, and inhaled deeply.

"Emmm, that smells like Tina. Or wait, is that Keisha?" He inhaled again. "It don't matter. Whoever it was, it all smells and tastes the same." He smiled.

As Reginald scrutinized his latest bill from the new escort service, he wondered if he had a problem. He spent more and more money on phone sex and call girls. His last tryst was with two women.

He had to pay extra, but he told himself after all he had endured, he deserved two women.

That night, they drank, partied, and had the wildest sex three people could have. Reginald didn't need

Viagra, but he used it just as a backup. The girls seemed thrilled to have a man who could go the extra mile.

When one came, the other would step up and handle the job. He would've been right back at that escort company if he didn't have to meet with the old man.

Reginald was getting tired of the sex scandals and everything else going on at Sweetwater. He now viewed the church as just another job, and like most employees, he was happiest when he was far, far away from work.

He nearly pissed himself when his father barged his way into his office. Reginald couldn't put the bills away fast enough.

His hands trembled as he looked up at his father.

"What the hell are you in here doing?" Pastor Goodlove screamed. "You should be making arrangements for my meeting with the church later, not in here shuffling papers!"

"Gee, what's there to prepare for? You said you wanted to talk to the congregation, and we called a special meeting. You get up, you talk," Reginald said.

He just couldn't sit still under his father's close stare. Pastor Goodlove refused to take a seat. Instead, he stood hovering over Reginald.

"I need an update on the expansion. What have you been doing? Did you go back down there yet?" Reginald shook his head.

"I didn't get a chance to go yet. I was just about to call the developer and try to see if he could—"

"What? You must think I'm some kinda fool. Boy, you wasn't doing nothing but shuffling papers when I walked up in here. You wasn't about to call a soul. And what do you mean 'call to try to see'? Am I paying for this expansion? Is that my hard-earned money, the money Sweetwater members have entrusted me with?"

Reginald just nodded, praying the tirade would soon be over.

"Then I suggest you pick up that phone, call whomever you need to, and tell them you're coming down there this evening!" the pastor snapped.

"But, I had, um—"

"You had what? You had a better idea of how to earn your salary? Is that what you're trying to tell me?"

Reginald gave up. There was simply no point in even trying to explain himself. He'd let the pastor holler, scream, and throw things even. It was just easier that way.

Going to Victoria was the last thing he wanted to do, but he knew it would do him very little good to argue.

"OK, Gee, if you want me down in Victoria this evening, then I'll go."

"You're damn right you'll go."

Reginald just wanted him to leave. Maybe he could call one of his girlfriends and have her come along for the ride. That's exactly what he'd do. The minute Gee left, he'd do it up in style.

Pastor Goodlove couldn't leave his son's office fast enough. When he did leave, Reginald took a deep breath and picked up the phone.

Once his plans were set, he called the car service they used and asked to be picked up at his place. He had already arranged his date, and Candy was more than happy about taking her job on the road.

* * *

Barry was nervous and confused. He was upset and nearly drunk. He had no idea how he had found himself in such a mess. How was he going to deal with Sissy? At night when he closed his eyes and begged sleep to come quickly, he still heard her voice shrieking, "You'll be sorry!" Then, just before he woke each morning, that same voice greeted him in his head.

The anticipation of what she would do sent a shock of sheer panic through his veins. He feared her for so many reasons; he couldn't believe how he had once fallen weak to her advances.

His relationship with Amy wasn't supposed to go this way. At first he thought he'd test the waters to make sure he still had it, then break away and marry the girl of his dreams. He knew he should've stayed away, but once Sissy started flirting, he became flattered, then curious. Before he knew it, he found himself having feelings for her too; but he knew those feelings were nothing more than lust. Barry admitted to himself that his feelings for Sissy were more like a courteous friendship. He knew he was wrong, but it was his moment of weakness, and it shouldn't last a lifetime. He just wished he knew what Sissy was up to.

"Oh-o, what have I done?" he asked, as he poured himself another drink. The incidents with Sissy ramming the car, then showing up at his place were definitely his way out. But a part of him didn't welcome the excuse he had prayed for only a month earlier. Why did she have to threaten him?

As the strong liquor sent a warm path down his throat, he poured himself another drink.

When the phone rang, he looked toward it and went back to his somber celebration. Its continuous ring reminded him that his machine wasn't on. He snatched it from its cradle.

"Yeah?" he screamed.

"Babe?" Amy's sweet voice had an instant calming effect on him. "Is everything OK? I thought you'd be happy to hear from me. We're baaaack," she sang playfully.

"Oh, I'm sorry. I've been getting a bunch of crank calls." Barry hiccupped.

"Are you sure you're OK?"

"Em hmm. I'm cool," he slurred.

"I don't know what's going on, but I'm on my way over," she said.

Barry couldn't come up with a good enough excuse for why she shouldn't, so he just dropped the phone and drained his glass.

Amy had a wholesome, charmed look. She was petite and wore her hair in a short and straight pageboy haircut. Her smile was dazzling, with sparkling white teeth. She had the deepest set of dimples Barry had ever seen.

She fell into his arms the moment he stumbled to the front door.

"Eeewww, you reek of alcohol. When did you start drinking? A girl goes away for a month, and her fiancé goes off the deep end." She giggled.

Barry could hardly stand up straight. She kissed him passionately, then pulled back.

"Hey, why are you sitting up here having a pity party all by yourself?"

This was the moment of truth for Barry. He closed his eyes, rubbed his face, and yawned.

"We gotta have a serious talk."

"OK." Amy blinked. Barry tried his best to sit upright. He cleared his throat and began.

"OK, remember that one time when we did, well, you know," he said.

Amy's body began to shake. Her eyes pooled with tears and she started wringing her hands.

"I have asked God for forgiveness for that. We're going to be married soon, and we won't have to worry about that. It was a moment of weakness, but it never happened again," she said.

Again Barry sighed.

"My parents would be devastated if they ever found out. Remember how my father counseled us about remaining true to God's Word? I just don't want to think about it, Barry.

"Besides, we've done good. We haven't succumbed to the flesh again. My body is a temple." Amy stopped talking when Barry's hand went up.

He shook his head. "Please, let me do this while I still have the courage. I am so sorry," he said. A frown creased her forehead.

"Oh my goodness. What have you done?"

Barry started crying. He didn't deserve Amy. He knew he wasn't good enough for her. He had long known he wouldn't be able to live up to her high standards.

"Somehow, a tape of us that day got out. Now someone is blackmailing me, threatening to show it to your church and mine," he mumbled.

Amy fainted.

That's when Barry knew for sure, he had to do whatever it took to keep this mess with Sissy a secret.

CHAPTER 19

"I say let he who is without sin cast the first stone!" Pastor Goodlove looked toward the crowd. "You see, we don't know what that young man is going through. But Sweetwater, I'm telling you, this is only the devil at work. Only Lucifer himself would use a troubled young man to spread such vile words about a man of God!" He shook his head as he spoke.

The parishioners sat riveted to their seats. This was what they needed. This was why they'd come to his church above all others. No one could deliver the word quite like their pastor.

"We don't want you to ever leave us," someone cried.

"The devil himself would have to pry my cold, stiff hands away from my family here," the pastor said. He was grateful for the support, but he wanted to remain on course. He didn't want to get sidetracked.

"We are just gonna have to be the Christians we are, and wrap our arms around this young man. He's troubled, but that's just the devil. He's still family."

"But what about the others?" a voice asked.

At first, the pastor didn't know if he should respond. He kept speaking, moving around like he used to do during his Sunday morning sermons. Until he heard it again, that voice. He looked in the direction he thought he heard it come from, but didn't see anyone who could've been the culprit. Pastor Goodlove shook his head.

"I want to thank you, Sweetwater, for your support. Just bear with me during this turmoil, and know that I am with you, and here for you."

He was preparing to step down from the platform when the words stopped him cold in his tracks.

"I think we should go to the board about whether you should continue to lead this church."

The pastor did a double-take, squinted, and tried to see if he could figure out where the voice was coming from. All he saw were smiling faces, looking back at him adoringly.

He hadn't given thought to the members going to the board. It was definitely an option, one that he himself had voted for before taking over for his late father. But never once did he think the possibility would ever loom over his head.

Pastor Goodlove couldn't fathom life without being at the head of one of Houston's most powerful and influential houses of worship. Sweetwater Powerhouse of God was him and he was it.

No, they wouldn't, they couldn't, he told himself as he slipped into his chambers.

Theola had been sitting in her normal spot on the front pew. For the first time in a long while she felt scared. What if the board members voted Ethan out as pastor of Sweetwater? What would that mean for their lifestyle? She didn't even want to consider the possibilities.

She decided against chasing behind him. Theola didn't like problems. She was no longer made for the struggle, and she knew it. When she agreed to marry a man old enough to be her father, she did so for security.

Now all of these so-called Christians were about to jeopardize the very fabric of her comfortable life? She looked over at Mama Sadie and the holy rollers with sheer hatred in her eyes. She had grown to hate everything about them. She didn't like the way they sat around talking about everyone who didn't dress, walk, or talk the way they liked, or even people who didn't pray or worship the way they saw fit.

Theola had a feeling that Mama Sadie and her crew were somehow behind the campaign to bring her husband down. She had to give the old lady credit, though. Either she was real tough or too stupid to know when she should sit her tail down.

Just as Theola stared at her with a frown across her face, Mama Sadie started staring right back. She wasn't even attempting to retreat. Theola shook her head and the old woman had the nerve to give her the finger! That only went to prove the old woman was teetering on the verge of insanity as far as Theola was concerned.

Theola turned her head quickly to see if anyone else had witnessed it; she couldn't believe it. How could these people put themselves on a moral pedestal the way they did?

She sucked her teeth and started to gather her belongings. She needed to get as far away from

Sweetwater as humanly possible. But she wasn't about to give up the fight.

On her way out, she vowed that if Mama Sadie and the holy rollers wanted a battle, then they'd better come prepared to fight. Because there was no way Theola Goodlove was about to go back to the bleak life she once knew, and she certainly wasn't about to do so because a bunch of meddling old ladies didn't know their place.

CHAPTER 20

It didn't take long for Pastor Goodlove to find out who had made the comments during his talk with members of Sweetwater. It had been Deacon Parker, a big man who thought he should hold far more power in the church than he did.

Unfortunately for Pastor Goodlove, Deacon Parker had been quite persuasive in his attempts to overthrow Sweetwater's leader.

Sources didn't hesitate to inform the pastor that the board had agreed to convene and meet to discuss his problems and how they should impact his position at Sweetwater PG.

Pastor Goodlove sat listening intently, but not really worried. He knew no one could lead Sweetwater the way he did, and he hoped the congregation realized that as well.

As he sat thinking about Deacon Parker, he wondered why the peasant of a man had never surfaced on his radar before now. Either way, if the deacon thought Pastor Goodlove was going to lay in waiting like a sitting duck, well, he had another thing coming.

One of the first things the pastor planned to do was have Reginald review the bylaws to see if he was able to be present during the board's hearing. Once that was determined, he'd make sure he came prepared.

Sitting at his desk, Pastor Goodlove couldn't imagine how he found himself in such a terrible situation. But he was not about to allow that situation to dictate him or his future. He got up, ready to leave.

He knew that his was a future that involved him at the helm of Sweetwater.

He was just about to turn off the TV in his office when the news came on. What he saw forced him right back down in his chair.

The pastor looked up to see Maurice's somber face on the screen. Two men were by his side. He suspected they were his attorneys. He sat there in disbelief as he listened to the men take turns trashing his good name.

"The truth of this situation is, we have a well-respected man of the cloth who is charged with holding morality to the highest esteem, and here he is taking advantage of vulnerable young men." The other man spoke.

"You have to remember these young men are looking to him for spiritual guidance. They're not soliciting sex. They see this man as someone they can run to for help and confide in when needed, and he takes that trust and turns it into something vile."

Pastor Goodlove shook his head at the screen. He was not about to sit back and allow his good name to be dragged through the mud!

CHAPTER 21

Pastor Goodlove sat behind his large desk. He sighed and wondered how it had come to this. His head was hurting, but it was the pain in his heart that bothered him the most. Every time he thought about the formal letter that was sent by registered mail to Blueridge, he got sick to his stomach.

The letter informed him that the Sweetwater Powerhouse of God's executive board would hold a meeting in two weeks. At that time he, Pastor Ethan Ezeekel Goodlove III, would be asked to make an appearance to answer specific questions. Two weeks after the hearing, the board would organize a vote for members of the congregation, who would then decide if Pastor Goodlove should be impeached.

Pastor Goodlove allowed his mind to linger to thoughts of a possible impeachment.

After hot, steamy sex in the shower with Damien, Jazzlyn was completely spent. She looked over at his sleeping body and wondered why he had to make things so difficult.

They were so good together. She vowed to wait him out, knowing he was just confused. If only she could get Michelle to leave her man alone, they'd be able to get through the rough patch and make plans for the future—their future, together.

It hadn't been easy to convince Damien to see her again, but she had pulled it off. When she saw him at that restaurant with that other woman, if you could even call her that, Jazzlyn was determined to go home with him instead. When the woman got up and went to the bathroom, she moved in for the kill.

She told Damien she was sorry for all of the nasty things she said. Once the police dropped the charges against her, she explained that they had found another suspect, and she realized Damien had nothing to do with the whole arrest thing.

It didn't take long for Jazzlyn to figure out that Michelle would be the target of the investigation. So that meant when she was eventually arrested, jailed, and convicted, Damien would be single again, and Jazzlyn wanted to be ready.

When the woman walked out of the bathroom and saw Jazzlyn all up under Damien, she stood in front of the table and gazed down at them.

"What the hell?" the stranger asked.

Damien, who had been drinking, looked up and smiled.

Jazzlyn couldn't believe her good fortune. She simply looked up at the woman and said, "You know he's a married man. I'm a good friend of the family." The woman grabbed her purse and dashed out of the restaurant.

Damien had forgiven Jazzlyn, so she immediately told him it was time for the best make-up sex he'd ever experienced.

Hours later, when Damien's cell phone rang from the hotel's outer room and he didn't stir, a light went off in Jazzlyn's head. She allowed the phone to ring a couple more times before she decided to answer it.

Jazzlyn walked out of the room and picked up the cell phone.

"Hello?" After a few seconds of silence she considered hanging up. The voice was faint.

"Ah, hello?"

"Yes?" Jazzlyn said. "Um, who is this? Michelle?"

"This is?" She could sense the anger in Michelle's voice.

"Why are *you* answering Damien's cell phone?" Michelle demanded to know.

"The question should be why are you *calling* his cell phone. Besides, we're in bed and he's not available right now," Jazzlyn bragged.

"Jazzlyn, you must think I'm a fool. If you and Damien are in bed, how could you, why would you even bother answering the phone?"

Jazzlyn paused for a moment. She looked toward the bedroom, then lowered her voice.

"Look, Michelle, Damien told me it was over between the two of you. Now I've invested a lot of time, and I have no intention of walking away from all of my hard work . . . you know, the way you did? Honey, he's not available. We're going to work this out. You're just wasting your time."

"Bitch, if you don't put Damien on the phone . . ." Michelle hissed.

"You're going to do what? You had your chance;

you lost him. I don't think he would want to talk to the woman who couldn't keep him happy. Besides, we know what you did, and soon you'll get yours!"

Jazzlyn waited to hear a response from Michelle. When she didn't get one, she continued.

"The truth is, Michelle, as far as I'm concerned, Damien Goodlove's heart is up for grabs. And honestly, between you and me, I think your time has passed. You need to move aside and let a real woman step in and do what you couldn't—keep him happy."

"You lowly skank! Do you think you could keep Damien happy? He ain't nothing but a big ole nasty freak just like you! You wasn't woman enough to get your own man, so you zeroed in on the biggest ho you could find! I need to speak to him now!"

Jazzlyn wanted to scream. She could hardly contain the venom boiling in the pit of her stomach. She couldn't believe what she was hearing.

"A skank? A nasty freak? Not woman enough to get a man? Girl, puhleeze! I took yours! Now what?"

"You watch too many damn soap operas. Look, you didn't take my man, I left the clown, so you can have fun with my sloppy seconds. Damien and you are meant to be together, and honestly, I pity you."

Jazzlyn began rubbing the knot that surfaced near her shoulder.

Michelle spat, "Now put my soon-to-be ex-husband on the phone before I come over there and beat your ass!"

"Oh whatever, Michelle. If it's so over between you two, why are you still calling? Obviously he doesn't want to be with you anymore. That's why he's here with me."

"Jazzlyn, Damien and I have children together,

you fool. Put him on the phone. It's an emergency. I don't have time for this mess. And you can have him!"

"If you were doing your job, he wouldn't be here with me in the first place."

"Jazzlyn! I don't care! Just wake the punk up and put him on the phone!" Michelle cleared her throat. "Besides, I'm willing to bet that sooner or later, he's going to do to you the exact same thing he did to me!"

"Oh, I don't think so," Jazzlyn bragged. "See, there's a big difference between me and you. Um, it's like with you he was settling for bronze when he could get the gold with me!"

Jazzlyn rubbed her temple. She couldn't believe Michelle's unrelenting denial.

"Look, Michelle, I'd like to finish this conversation, but it's not going anywhere. Besides, I think I just heard my man. I want to be at his side when he wakes up."

She pushed the end button on the cellular phone before Michelle could respond. When she turned to go back into the bedroom, Damien was standing there. Jazzlyn froze.

His silence said everything he was probably feeling. Her first instinct was to toss the cell phone. But it was obvious Damien had seen it, and heard her on it. Jazzlyn looked down at the phone in her hand and suddenly felt like a child caught being naughty.

"What the hell are you doing on my cell phone? Why would you invade my privacy by answering my cell phone?"

Jazzlyn lowered her gaze to the floor. She felt her throat go dry. How could she respond? How could she answer the question? She wanted desperately to take back the events as they unfolded only moments ago.

"It rang and you were sleeping." Jazzlyn looked up, but not at him. "Ah, it could've been important?" She hoped that would be a sufficient explanation, but knew it wouldn't cut it.

When Damien moved to the sofa and sat down, her heart dropped. Just when she felt they had been making progress, the desperate feelings that crept up on her the night she accused him of having her arrested had returned.

"Look, I think we should cool it a bit. I mean—"

"What are you saying?" Jazzlyn felt herself get warm. "Didn't last night mean anything to you?"

"I'm just not ready for this kind of stuff again," Damien said.

"But I thought we'd get married now." She looked down. "You know, now that it's over between you and Michelle. She just told me she didn't want you anymore."

"What!" Damien snatched the cell phone. "That was Michelle on the phone? You stupid bitch. What did you say to my wife?"

Reginald told the driver to pull over at a rest stop off Highway 59 south, about fifteen miles outside of Victoria. Candy had been grinding on his leg and talking dirty in his ear for the past hour. He had caught the driver Darren sneaking glances through the rear-view mirror.

The thought made Reginald feel like a man of real power. He had something another man wanted.

Candy's short skirt did wonders for her long legs. The fact that she didn't bother putting panties on made it all the more interesting.

The last time Reginald caught Darren sneaking a peek, he palmed Candy's bare ass and winked at the driver. Shortly after when they stopped for gas, he got out of the car.

"Aeeey, you like Candy?" Reginald asked the driver as he walked around to where he stood.

Darren looked away from Reginald.

"It's OK, man. I ain't my father. Trust me, she's a hot piece of ass, too."

Darren smiled at Reginald. He seemed to relax a bit.

"You're a lucky man, Mr. Goodlove. Very lucky!" Darren said.

"Hmm, I got a lot of women like her. And trust me, all of them aim to please, just like her."

"Wow! Must be nice," Darren said again, shifting his eyes away from Reginald. "You know, I've always liked you, Mr. Goodlove. You're cool."

Reginald stuck his chest out a little farther. No one had ever called him "cool" before.

"You know I like you too, Darren. That's why I told Pops he needed to hire you full time."

"What! That was you, man? Aeey, thanks so much. I love working for the Gee man," Darren said.

"How far away are we?" Reginald asked.

"I'd say we're about thirty minutes away. The little lady getting restless?" Darren asked.

"Oh, even if she was, she ain't saying a word. That's how I got 'em. Hey, I have an idea, why don't you find a rest stop to pull over and we'll see if maybe we can't introduce you to Candy."

Darren removed the gas hose from the car. He stepped closer to Reginald.

"What are you saying?"

"I'm saying I don't mind sharing. I'll let you get a little taste." Reginald grinned.

"You're joking, right?"

Reginald shook his head.

"But what's she gonna say about that?"

"Man, I told you, I handles mine. You just find a rest stop. I'll keep her warm for you."

Once he found a spot, Darren steered the car off into the rest stop. He found the last parking spot he could find and turned off the engine.

Reginald got out of the car and Candy followed closely behind. They walked around to the driver's side of the car.

When Darren rolled down his window, Candy licked her lips.

"Reggie tells me you got the hots for me. Is that true?"

Darren smiled.

"Well, he has a great idea. Why don't the three of us go over there to the restroom and see if we can't get better acquainted? Would you like that?"

The smile that crept across Darren's face made Reginald proud.

On what should've been a relaxing day at a spa— having her nails, hair, and makeup done—Sissy was instead wearing out the carpet in her bedroom.

"So Barry Goodlove thinks he can just drop me now that his little Ms. Homemaker is back? Hmm!"

She paced the floor from the bathroom to the

bed, her mind constantly thinking about her next move and how she could make Barry's life a living hell.

That had quickly become her new mission. It didn't take long for her to determine she had to do something to somehow make up for the humiliation she felt with each number she dialed.

It was the phone call to her mother that had the most impact. She couldn't get that conversation out of her mind, and that was the one that all but convinced her she'd have to do something to fix Barry and his little Ms. Prissy, Amy.

"Hey, Juanita." Sissy rolled her eyes when she heard her mother sigh.

"Sissy, wait. Don't tell me you're knocked up and that's why we're rushing this wedding. Well, I sure can't wait to see this high falutin', fancy, church-goin' family you 'bout to marry into." Juanita chuckled.

"That's not why I'm calling," Sissy said.

"Oh?"

"The wedding's off," Sissy quickly blurted out.

"Hhmm, I knew that was gonna happen. I told you it wouldn't last, didn't I? Hmmm, found yourself a good Christian man and couldn't keep your legs closed, huh? You should learn to listen. I've been there and done that. When I raised you girls to marry preachers, I shoulda told you that you can't treat them like regular mens," Juanita said.

Sissy rolled her eyes.

"And to imagine, you thought you could make that marriage work? Hmm, you couldn't even make it to the altar. I may have been married once or twice but—"

"Juanita, you've been married six times," Sissy

interrupted. "And let's not forget, you never quite made it all the way up to a preacher. There was the Sunday school teacher, two ushers—"

"Least I did so on my terms!" Juanita hissed, cutting her daughter off. "When you can land yourself a husband, then you can try to tell me about my affairs. You wait till after I bought those tickets, then call to say you ain't getting married at all? Huh, I sure hope you plan on reimbursing me for them," Juanita whined.

"Juanita, I paid for your ticket and Kelly's too, remember?"

"Well, you should give me something for making plans to come there. Now I'm left holding the bag."

"Juanita, remember I wanted you guys to come early, but you gave me some excuse why you needed to fly in the day before and leave as soon as the wedding was over?"

Sissy could hear her mother sucking in the cigarette that always hung between her lips.

"Look, Juanita, I need to run," she said.

"Well, thanks for nothing. Next time you decide to get hitched, why don't you just call after the deed is done? Then send me an e-mail and I'll just forward the bad news to everyone in my address book."

Before Sissy could respond, the dial tone started ringing in her ear. Now, as she paced and reviewed her conversation with Juanita, something the bitter old hag said gave her just the idea she needed.

She lay back and smiled at the plan that was sure to teach Barry and Amy a lesson.

CHAPTER 22

"So, when I say it's important to make love . . . I say it's important to make love in the right position, I'm only telling you what God intended!" Pastor Goodlove paused and looked out at the congregation. "It's important to make love in the right position!"

He moved away from the pulpit. The blanket of sweat was already drenching his body.

"You see, sex is God's Idea. It's a holy act. But people are abusing it and misusing it!" Pastor Goodlove looked again at the congregation. "Hello, somebody!"

"Sex is a holy act. God created it for marriage." He shuffled to one side of the church and looked into a young woman's eyes. "Your body is a temple for the Holy Ghost." He pointed at another young woman.

"Stop spending quality time with unqualified people!"

"Amen, Pastor!" the crowd cheered.

"Those unqualified people will try to violate your temple! They will lead you to believe there's nothing wrong with casual sex! Ahha!" He skipped to the other end of the church. "But I'm here to tell you,

God created sex to inaugurate marriage and for no
other reason."

Several people jumped to their feet.

"Huh, I know it feels good. But everything that
feels good ain't good for ya!" the pastor screamed.

"Hallelujah, Pastor. Preach!"

"See, many of us, we treat—well, not me." He
chuckled.

Most members joined in his laughter.

"I say, many of us, we treat sex and food just alike
. . . when we're hungry, we go out and get us some!"

"Preach, Pastor! You betta preach!"

Pastor Goodlove waited for the thunderous ap-
plause to die down.

"So when I say there is danger in making love in
the wrong position . . . better understand, God says
the right, the only position is being married!"

The organ started up, Mama Sadie began her rou-
tine, and the pastor ran from the pulpit, leaving Sweetwater's members finally fulfilled. With the pending
impeachment hearing looming, Pastor Goodlove felt
it was time for him to go back to the pulpit.

Michelle was hoping to duck in and out of church
without being noticed. Her main reason for showing
up was to try to catch her husband and his new
woman. But instead of seeing him, her two friends
saw her.

"Girl, where you been hiding?" Tammy asked.

"Oh, I've been trying to get my life in order."

"Emph, and you feel like you gotta do that alone?"
Kim countered.

She didn't feel like putting a bunch of people all

up in her business. Even though Kim and Tammy were her girls, they were still members of Sweetwater.

"So, what's up with you and Damien? We ain't seen him in a minute," Tammy said.

"Nothing really. I haven't seen him since we separated."

Kim reached over and hugged Michelle before she could do anything.

"Are you OK, girl?"

Fighting back tears she didn't realize she was harboring, Michelle removed herself from Kim's embrace.

"Why don't we all go to brunch so we can talk?" Tammy suggested.

"I wish I could, but I need to go meet with the Gee man. That's why I came."

"Girl, you hear that sermon this morning? Making love in the right position! Ooooh, it is so good to have the pastor back where he belongs."

"Yeah, he can count on my vote. If it was up to me, he wouldn't even be going through this mess," Kim confirmed.

"What mess?" Michelle had been so wrapped up in her own problems that she wasn't even aware of what was going on at Sweetwater.

"Girl, the board is having an impeachment hearing. They're gonna do a vote on whether we should keep the pastor." Michelle jumped back.

"Impeachment?" She frowned.

"Yes, girl, it's all people are talking about. Well, I know how I'm voting. The board members are walking around here telling us not to discuss it amongst ourselves. I'm like, I will talk to whoever, whenever, wherever, and however I like," Kim hissed.

"Wait, you're telling me the board is going to try to impeach Pastor Goodlove?"

"The vote is next Sunday evening right after service. They're gonna announce the results at Bible study on Wednesday," Kim explained.

Michelle felt lost. She was about to go talk to Pastor Goodlove about Damien and Jazzlyn, but knowing what he was going through, she decided her problems could wait.

As she made a dash for her car, she saw Theola sitting in hers. Michelle looked around the parking lot, then walked over.

She tapped on her window.

"Looks like you could use a friend," she said.

"You think Ninfa's is open on a Sunday afternoon?" Theola asked.

"Girl, if it's not, we can find someplace that is. Follow me?"

CHAPTER 23

Pastor Goodlove had been smiling at the constant stream of visitors after his sermon. Most of the parishioners wanted to personally tell him that he could count on their vote of support the following week.

A part of him wanted to remind his congregation of just what they'd be missing out on if they voted him out as their leader.

He also made a passionate plea for members to remain loyal in their financial commitments. By the end of his sermon, the sanctuary looked like the good old days.

Just as he thought he was closing his office door for some much needed rest, Mama Sadie and her crew approached.

"A moment of your time, Pastor?"

"For you, ladies, as much as you need," he said, opening the door wide enough for them to come in.

"We won't take up too much of your time," Mama Sadie began. Before Pastor Goodlove could sit down, she began. "We have talked amongst ourselves, Pastor. We have decided to let you know just where we stand with this impeachment hearing. We are willing to sway the vote your way if you'll agree to our conditions."

Pastor Goodlove could hardly believe his ears. He looked at Mama Sadie and the rest of her followers.

"Are you trying to bribe me?" he asked.

"I wouldn't go to that extreme," Mama Sadie said. She looked at him. "Are you interested in hearing us out, or do you wanna risk it?"

When he didn't answer, she extended her hand toward Ms. Geraldine.

"Our demands, or um, requests are simple really. First off, we'd like you to get rid of Theola. We don't like her, and we don't think you do either. Next, there's the issues with your sons. We want you to push up the wedding between Barry and that Amy, because Sweetwater could use some new blood in here. Lastly, we want to take part in the selection of Sweetwater's next first lady. It's obvious that like most men, Pastor, when left to handle such a delicate matter yourself, you think with the wrong head. I'm not sure where you found Theola, but she's not right for Sweetwater."

"And if I don't agree to your requests?"

"Well, you take your chances against impeachment."

Several days had passed since Damien caught Jazzlyn with his cell phone. Still, Damien fumed when he thought of the startled look plastered across her face. Sitting across from Barry with a cold brew in his hand, he was trying to calm down.

"So, what did she say when you caught her, red-handed at that?" Barry asked.

"What could she say, man? I heard her talking crap to Michelle. But that wasn't the point. The point was, she answered my cell phone. I don't play that snooping shit."

Barry nodded as Damien continued to speak.

"That's the kind of mess I hate about most women. They're so insecure. I can't live like that, you know what I mean?"

"Yeah, man, I understand."

"You should've seen the look on her face when she turned around and saw me standing in the doorway."

"Man, you have the best stories. But I guess when you got so many women, there's probably a lot to tell. I can't even begin to wrap my imagination around the situation you're in." Barry shook his head. "And you got it all under control."

"Barry, it's really not like that, man."

"Yeah, tell me anything," Barry said. "But seeing is believing, and from what I see, you definitely got it like that, man."

The knock at the door put their conversation on hold.

"You wanna get that? I need to grab something to eat. Besides, I'm not expecting company," Barry said as he rose from his seat closest to the kitchen.

When Damien opened the door, he was a bit surprised to see Jazzlyn standing there. She was wearing a long coat that she clutched to her chest.

"Can I come in?" she asked. He stepped aside.

"I don't think that's such a good idea. How'd you find me here anyway?"

Jazzlyn eased in and dropped the coat to the floor.

Damien turned to see her standing in a pair of high heels and a matching bra and panty set.

"Ah, I was about to leave anyway. I need to go check my e-mail. My computer is down and at the repair shop. Um, I told the guy I'd come see about it today," Barry said as he put down the glass he was holding. He grabbed his keys and left.

Barry was about to stop at the computer shop when his cell phone rang. He could hardly make out what Amy was saying because she was crying and sobbing so hard.

He quickly turned his car around and rushed over to her place.

"What happened?" he asked, struggling to control his out-of-control heartbeat. He quickly turned the car around and zoomed toward Amy's place.

He had arrived in little time. When he got there, Amy was even more upset than she sounded over the phone.

"I was logging on to check my e-mails when one in particular caught my eye. Everyone else's e-mail address was hidden except mine. I couldn't tell who sent it, but the title made me curious."

She pointed toward the screen. When Barry looked, his heart dropped.

"Amy, You Finally Won!!!" the subject line screamed.

Amy tried to pace her fingers to match his reading.

Yes, you won . . . Your hard work has paid off! I hope you are finally happy. You have thrown yourself at Barry Goodlove relentlessly. Barry and I were look-

ing forward to a wonderful life together, but now, thanks to you and your deliberate efforts to undermine our love, he jilted me at the alter. YES, WE WERE SUPPOSED TO GET MARRIED AT SWEETWATER POWERHOUSE OF GOD, his daddy's church. I hope you are proud. It's women like you who give us all a very bad name. Not only am I out of tens of thousands of dollars for canceling our wedding at the very last minute, but my heart is shattered. I try to understand how one woman can do this to another and not feel an ounce of remorse, but I've come to realize and understand that in your selfish quest, your bitterness won't allow you to see the mere possibility of anyone else's happiness. This devastation has left both my family and me in distress.

So, Amy Blackwell at Amy@yahoo.com, you no longer have to drive by my house in the wee hours of the morning to see if his car is parked here. It won't be. You no longer have to hang up once you hear my voice for the sixth time in any given hour, after you sit and call my home over and over again. You will now know where to find him. You don't have to question my neighbors about whether they've seen him around. He won't come anymore.

I am sending this e-mail out in hopes that some other woman who is conniving enough to try to lure a man away might think twice about feelings other than her own. I hope that people are so disturbed by your behavior that they bombard both you and Barry with countless e-mails and phone calls. Again, congrats Amy Blackwell at Ablackwell@HPBI.com, daughter of BISHOP HOWARD BLACKWELL OF HOUSTON'S PREMIER BIBLICAL INSTITUTE, and

BARRY GOODLOVE, son of ETHAN EZEEKEL GOODLOVE III, Bgoodlove@SPG.com, I hope you two are happy. You deserve each other!

Amy blinked, then looked at Barry.

"She cannot be serious!" she screamed. Before he could read it again, the phone rang. Amy picked it up before it could ring a second time.

"Um. Yes, I am at my computer, but Barry is here right now. Can I call you back?"

She looked at Barry. He felt awful.

"No, I really need to call you back. I promise I will. Yes, I read the e-mail. Mother, that's my other line. Hold one sec." Amy clicked over.

"Hello?" She shook her head. "Hi, Daddy. Mom's on the other line. Can I call you back?" she asked. She looked Barry directly in the eyes.

"OK, I'll call you when I'm done with Mom." She sobbed and clicked over to the other line.

When Amy clicked back to tell her mother she'd call her later, there was silence. A few seconds later her mother clicked back on the line.

"Mother," Amy said. She stopped talking. "Yes, I got the e-mail. That was Daddy on the other line."

"Aunt Rose too?" Amy asked.

"I can't believe Sissy would stoop this low," Barry mumbled.

"Can I call you back?" Amy asked her mother before she could say anything else.

After fielding calls from just about every relative she had in her online address book, Amy was tired and very upset.

The phone wouldn't stop ringing and she was getting tired of trying to explain. Finally, Amy gave up and simply took her phone off the hook. She looked at Barry, who was still reading the e-mail.

"How could she?" Amy asked.

Barry didn't know what to say. He felt sorry for Amy, and horrible that he had dragged her into this mess.

"Why does this woman think you were gonna marry her?" Amy mumbled. She looked at Barry's face.

What could he say? That he was weak and had succumbed to the flesh? He couldn't admit to himself that he had been unfaithful to Amy, and more importantly, he couldn't admit it to God.

Soon, his mind started racing with thoughts of who might've gotten that e-mail. When Amy returned to her computer, she had more than three hundred e-mails!

"Oh my, you see that? More than three hundred e-mails in a matter of minutes." She looked at Barry, then back to the screen.

Amy opened one e-mail and regretted it before she could push the delete button.

> *Amy,*
> *You don't know me, but I wanted to send you an e-mail to say women like you make me want to vomit. If it were legal to kill, you'd have to go into hiding. I suspect it was a woman just like you who stole my husband. That woman was right to send out that e-mail. I hope you and that dog of yours, Barry Good-love, rot in hell for what you've done!*

Barry was mortified. He and Amy peeked at two other e-mails, and that first one was pleasant compared to the others.

Barry didn't know what to do, or even what to say.

CHAPTER 24

The Sunday morning before the big vote, Pastor Goodlove considered not preaching. But he thought better of it, and was glad he had.

He had prayed and asked God to forgive his sins. A feeling of calm washed over him when he thought about the fact that he would be OK if the board was able to drum up enough votes for his impeachment.

Pastor Goodlove was wrapping up yet another moving sermon.

"So, how do you deal with emergencies? I said, are you like most? Do you dial 911, call for the police or the fire department? Or maybe you call on big mama?"

The congregation went wild again.

"You see, I know how you can deal with the terror in your life. The terrorist may be your boss at work, may be your neighbor next door, or may be that jealous coworker. Whoever it is, their objective is the same. The terrorist wants to kill, steal, destroy, and rob you of your joy! But I got a secret weapon!" The pastor jumped off the platform.

"Hallelujah, Pastor!"

"Preach, Pastor. Where is your secret weapon?"

"I saaaaid . . . got a secret weapon!" Pastor Goodlove chuckled and used the back of his hand to swoosh sweat from his brow.

"If you're gonna handle your own emergency, you need more than just a plan of action. You see, a plan of action, that's good. But I'm here to tell you, a secret weapon is even more effective!"

Pastor Goodlove fell to his knees. Mama Sadie was up and dancing, and the rest of the holy rollers were at her side.

"I said, my secret weapon is the one and only, the maker of all armor, the creator of everything protective, the almighty, glorious God Himself!"

The congregation shot to their feet.

"Preach, Pastor, preach!"

Pastor Goodlove looked at his congregation. "I've got my secret weapon. Do you?"

The organ started up and he eased his way back into his chambers.

Theola Goodlove was almost brought to tears as she watched her husband from the front pew. Once again, he had given the members just what they were longing for.

She glanced over at Mama Sadie, who was spread eagle on the floor. Other holy rollers surrounded her.

Theola hadn't forgotten her vow to make them pay. And she had no intentions of changing her mind.

She and Michelle had talked about their lives and problems within the church, and both agreed if the holy rollers were gone, Sweetwater could once again become a pleasant place to worship.

Theola told herself the money she was spending would pay off tenfold. She sat back and watched the drama unfold with the holy rollers laying a white sheet over Mama Sadie's Holy Ghost-filled body.

She shook her head, got up, and walked out after tithes and offerings.

CHAPTER 25

Pastor Goodlove was making sure his office was in order. He looked around and decided to call his driver so that he and his wife could go have brunch.

But before Theola arrived at his door, he opened it to find his attorneys standing there.

"I believe we might have something to make this awful mess go away."

David Swanson walked in, and his assistant followed closely behind.

"We've already discussed this with Reginald. He says to run it by you, and if you agree, I believe we can close the chapter on what's been a terrible time for you."

Pastor Goodlove looked at the men, but he didn't want to appear too hopeful. Before he could hear what the attorneys had to say, there was loud banging on his door.

"Excuse me for a moment," he said. The pastor pulled open the door.

"Pastor, so sorry to interrupt." Ms. Geraldine was nearly out of breath. "But there are several TV stations outside the church. Two of the reporters just tried to barge their way in. Somehow they found out about the vote." David stood.

"There's nothing we can do about it. If you don't want to speak, you don't have to, but it would be nice if you had a church spokesperson. That way they would get a comment. If you don't tell them something, those sharks will just make up what they want."

"You're suggesting I talk to them?"

David held out his hands.

"That's not what I said. I said you might want to have someone act as a spokesperson, just to explain the very basics. Yes, we are having a private board meeting. Yes, the congregation has been asked to vote. Then the person leaves and comes back inside. Simple."

Pastor Goodlove wasn't sure if talking to the press was a good idea. They had already run numerous stories about him, spreading untruths and ruining his name.

The other day one of the stations had an interview with the old deans of his seminary. Just as he was thinking about not talking to the press, he thought of Reginald. He'd be perfect.

Pastor Goodlove dialed his son's number.

"Reginald, I need you to hold a press conference. Get over here in ten minutes and bring a dark suit. Nothing cheap!" the pastor barked into the phone.

Damien felt like he had made progress. It wasn't anything huge, but still, when Jazzlyn showed up at Barry's door wearing next to nothing, he sent her packing. He really was through with her.

It wasn't an easy thing to do. While one head told him it was the right decision, the other disagreed by throbbing in frustrating pain.

But still he held his position. He didn't want to continue sleeping with Jazzlyn because it was clear she thought she was about to be the second Mrs. Goodlove, and he wasn't having that.

Damien decided to abandon his womanizing ways in hopes of helping his father with his crusade. When he walked out of Pastor Goodlove's chambers, he nearly bumped into Michelle.

"Oh, what's going on?" he asked.

Michelle's eyes narrowed when they zeroed in on him.

"I have been trying to get in touch with you for the longest. Look, you don't have to want me anymore, that's fine, but your daughter was in the hospital for an asthma attack and I couldn't even get your tired ass on the phone."

With her neck twisting and her hands on her hips, Michelle tried to push her way past him.

"Whoa!" He grabbed her arm and spun her around to face him. "Look, I know you're not happy with me, but Michelle, if you try to keep me from my daughters, I'm here to tell you that you're gonna have a fight on your hands. I'm not having it."

She looked at his hands, still on her arm, then looked him in the eyes.

"Don't even try it. You don't care about your kids or me! If you did, you wouldn't have left your family for some two-bit slut. But you know what, Dee, you can have her and she can have you! You two deserve each other." Michelle snatched her arm out of his clutch.

"I didn't even know you called." He looked down at the floor. He was embarrassed. "So Terry had an asthma attack? Is she OK? I'm sorry you couldn't reach me," he said.

Michelle stood in front of Damien.

"You can't make me believe that you care about us. I've been nothing but good to you. I cook, clean, fuck you when you want, but still it's never been enough for you. You just can't keep your pants zipped. Well, I'm tired. I'm sick and tired of your mess."

Damien wanted to say so much. He wanted to tell her he had no idea why he was the way he was. He wanted to tell her he'd go to counseling if she'd consider taking him back. But she wouldn't let up.

"I found your little scrapbook," she hissed.

"What scrapbook? What are you talking about?"

"You know, your collection of naked women posing in my lingerie. Don't act like you don't know what I'm talking about."

The comment took Damien by surprise. He wasn't sure how she found his stash, but then he remembered she had completely cleaned out their house.

"That was wrong what you did. Where are my things anyway? Did you put them in storage?"

Michelle looked at him and snickered.

"Your stuff?"

"Yeah. My suits, my electronics, my shoes, my stuff! What did you do with my things, Michelle?"

"Oh, I gave all of your shit to the Salvation Army. I figured I could help a real man make it in the world."

Damien slammed his hand into the wall.

"You better find my shit, Michelle. That's not even a little bit funny."

"Why don't you get Jazzlyn to buy you new clothes and shoes? Hmmm? I'm glad she's taking over, 'cause I'm tired of being played like some special kind of fool."

"Is my daughter OK? That's all I need to know. You can go about your business, and I'll be happy to give you a divorce, but I won't give up my kids no matter what you think." He stepped closer to her. "I'll fight you in court, and you know I'll win."

"You're a sick bastard. I mean, to have other women in your wife's lingerie is just nasty. You're nasty, they're nasty, and I'm through." Michelle started to walk away, but turned back to Damien. "If you even think about fighting me for custody, I'll pull out every nasty, scandalous thing you've ever done and parade your business all out in the streets. By the time I'm done with you, everybody in this church will know exactly what you are. And I do mean everybody, including your sick daddy." She stepped closer to him. "I guess they are right when they say the apple doesn't fall far from the tree."

Damien didn't even remember his hand leaving his side until he was pulling it back. Had he really slapped his wife? The look on her face soon answered his question.

The minute Michelle rubbed the side of her face, then frowned, he realized what he had done.

Before he could say he was sorry, she jumped on him, clawing at his face, neck, and chest. The shock of the attack sent him stumbling into the wall. Their bodies collided and tumbled to the floor.

Once on the ground, Michelle quickly straddled her husband and started delivering blows to his face and mid-section.

Damien was shocked. He tried to use his arms to protect his face.

"Girl, stop. Michelle, what the hell is wrong with you!" he screamed.

"You nasty, conniving snake!" WHOP! SMACK! "How dare you put," SMACK! WHOP! "your screwing hands on me! I'll kill you, you sleazy bastard!" she shrieked.

By now, a small crowd started approaching. But Michelle wouldn't let up. Damien was finally able to scoot away when two ushers pulled her off him while she continued to kick and scream. He sat on the floor wondering what had gotten into her.

Reginald was not happy about having to face the press. He just didn't feel like going out there and talking to reporters about church business. There was something so wrong with picking up the newspaper and reading about his father's sexcapades, then turning on the TV and having people actually talk about it.

When he arrived in the Gee man's office and saw the attorneys with their assistants busy at work, he knew he'd have to find something else to do. Yeah, the money was good, well, not the measly fifty thousand his father paid him yearly like it was six figures, but the extra he paid himself for all of the suffering and emotional abuse he had to endure. But Reginald was convinced he could do better. He could take his master's degree in finance and go work at a company that might pay him at least half of what he was worth. He'd finally be able to get away from the Gee man and all of his demands and problems.

"Boy, you hear me talking to you?"

Things were really getting bad as far as Reginald was concerned. Not only had he not heard what the old man said, but he didn't even want to be bothered.

"What?" Reginald snapped.

The room grew quiet. Pastor Goodlove rose from his chair. Veins started to protrude from his forehead and neck. He glared at Reginald and leaned forward on his desk.

"Who you talking to like that, boy?"

"I'm not a boy. I'm a man!" Reginald heard himself say. He was not sure why he chose that moment to stand up in defiance of his father, and he knew it wasn't the best move.

Pastor Goodlove deliberately walked from behind his desk and stopped in front of Reginald.

"Let's get this straight. You are what the fuck I say you are. I brought you into this world, and I won't hesitate to take you out! You will respect me!"

Reginald could feel the heat from his father's voice. He could also feel the other eyes staring them down.

"Now, I suggest you get yourself ready to go out there and talk to those reporters. And you'd better act like this is something you want to do. Do you understand me?"

Reginald didn't answer. He stood and stared at his father.

"Is there a problem?" Pastor Goodlove asked.

Again, Reginald stood silent.

"Now, with that taken care of, let's go over again what he should be saying," Pastor Goodlove said to the attorneys.

"I'm not saying shit, because I'm not going out there. I suggest you tell them what you want them to know."

For the second time in less than an hour, two members of the Goodlove family came to blows.

Sissy sat back and marveled at her brilliance and quick thinking. She was in awe when she thought about how easy it was to hack into both Barry and Amy's email accounts. Well, she didn't actually do it herself, but it didn't cost her much to pay the kid down the street for the instructions. For him it was nothing short of a challenge; he had even bet he could have it done in record time and he did.

Sissy had finally started feeling better about herself and that mess Barry had left in her lap. The beauty of her little plan was that she never put her name in the e-mail, so only those close to the doomed relationship would know it was actually her.

But Amy? Well, she had another thing coming. Sissy e-mailed everyone in Amy's personal and professional online address book, then did the same to Barry. If that wasn't enough, she posted the e-mail on various websites in Yahoo groups and other cyber spots.

She wondered what Barry was doing and whether he had seen the e-mail. A part of her also wondered if the members of Sweetwater PG had gotten it yet. She e-mailed them a copy of it too, then sent a copy to all of the other mega churches in Houston that had a website.

"Who cares?" she said as she got up from her sofa and strolled to the kitchen.

Sissy had extended the vacation she had taken for

her wedding since she knew she wouldn't be ready to return to work after bragging to everyone in the office about snagging the son of a prominent Houston minister. She'd also switched her membership to another church.

She wanted desperately to be a fly on the wall when those two strolled into church. She wasn't worried, because Sissy knew she could rely on her youth group contact for regular updates.

She thought back to their last conversation and was satisfied that just because she had left the church, that didn't mean she'd be out of the loop.

"Sissyyy, is that e-mail true?" Kenya had asked.

"It is. Can you believe it? I'm such a wreck over this," Sissy confirmed.

"Oh, I could just imagine. Well, if you need anything at all," Kenya said.

"Oh, I just need some time to deal with this. I could just imagine what it's been like at church lately," Sissy fished.

"You don't even want to know. I think everyone is secretly waiting for the two of them to come back. I heard Amy isn't even leaving to go to work. Her assistant said something about death threats. Our IT guy has complained that the system is being overloaded with e-mails. You know the staff didn't say who the e-mails were to, but, well, we all figured it out. Hell, I know for a fact that all of the ministry staff and assistants received an e-mail in their personal accounts. I've even heard some people were sending ten, even twenty e-mails, talking about that one everybody got. Can you imagine?"

Sissy struggled to contain her composure. She was absolutely delighted by the news.

"Oh." Kenya's voice dropped to a whisper. "I heard she and Barry may not be getting married! I don't know why or what happened, but that's the word floating around the church, girl."

"Really?" Sissy asked. Her voice was laced with fake concern.

"I'll try to see what I can find out and call you back. But for now, you try to get some rest, and don't worry about things around here. I'll call to check on you later, OK?"

"Hey, thanks, Kenya," Sissy had said.

She opened her refrigerator and pulled out a bottle of wine. Content that her plan was working on both fronts, Sissy turned her attention to what she might do next. She thought about calling other members of the church, just to see whether anyone suspected anything about Barry and Amy's sudden change in wedding plans.

Sissy dialed the number to Sweetwater's Youth Supervisor.

"Hello?" his baritone voice rang out.

"Heeey, Dougie. What's going on?"

"Who is this? Sissy?"

"Ah, yes it is," she sang.

"Oh, so I guess you finally got settled in over at your new church?"

"Kind of, but I miss you guys so much. What's going on these days?"

"The youth program is really looking up. We're about to start working on a few plays. We've got a lot coming up. It's a pity you had to leave," Douglass said.

"Yeah, it is," Sissy said. "So how's everyone else doing?" she inquired.

"Everybody is excited," Douglass reported.

"Well, I heard that Barry and that girl aren't getting married anymore. Is that true?"

"Sissy, you know I don't keep up with that kind of stuff. I'm not sure what's going on in people's personal lives," Douglass admitted calmly.

"Oh, I see. So you mean to tell me you haven't read that e-mail I heard is floating around there? Something about Barry and Amy?"

"Look, I'm a little busy. What is it exactly that you want, Sissy?" he asked.

"Oh, don't even worry about it," Sissy said. She slammed the phone back into its cradle.

She dialed Barry's number, and then threw the phone against the wall when his voicemail came on.

CHAPTER 26

Pastor Goodlove's eyes traveled over the twelve board members who sat before him. He had his attorneys at his side. Deacon Parker had the floor.

"Pastor Goodlove, we have entrusted you to guide us by example, but lately you have brought shame onto yourself, your family, and your family in Christ. We have heard your statements and what your attorneys have had to add to this. As you know, the bylaws state that you are to leave the room for thirty minutes while we vote. Once that vote is complete, we will take the issue to the congregation. We will give them a week to discuss and decide, and then their decision will be presented to the board. If we receive a decision which is made up of at least 50 percent of the congregation, then we follow that decision immediately and skip the second board meeting."

Deacon Parker glanced down at his notepad.

"If the board votes to impeach, we need at least fifty percent of the congregation to agree. If the board votes against impeachment, the congregation can still elect to do so. Is that clear?"

Pastor Goodlove couldn't believe the way he was

being treated. Of course he understood. He only
helped write the very bylaws that were being used
against him now.

"It is," he said.

"Do you have anything else to add before we close
the session and take a vote?"

"No." Pastor Goodlove stood and turned to leave
the room.

He and his attorneys walked back to his office to
wait for the verdict.

Theola couldn't believe it had come to this. She
didn't want to think the members of Sweetwater
would actually consider getting rid of the only leader
most of them ever knew.

But that's exactly what was happening. She was in
the sanctuary listening as the voting administrators
again went over the impeachment guidelines.

She glanced around the room to see that it was
standing room only. People who had not attended
Sweetwater in years seemed to go out of their way to
be there. She hoped that would turn out in her husband's favor.

Since the accusations came out, those who had
been pointing the finger had some questions to answer themselves.

Just two days ago, Maurice had to explain why he
had sued another pastor just before he graduated
from college. In that suit, he claimed he was forced
to perform oral sex against his will.

While the congregation was nearly divided over all
of the rumors that had been floating around, even
the pastor's toughest critics had to admit Maurice's
claims were suspect at best.

Theola straightened herself on the pew when Geraldine stood at the microphone.

"All praises to God almighty, Pastor Goodlove, the deacons, and good evening to all of you, my brothers and sisters in Christ." She looked out at the full room. "I wanted to take this time to remind you of the very important task at hand. You have the power to show your love, undying respect, and loyalty to our dear pastor."

Theola's head snapped toward the front of the church. Quite surely she was hearing things. Did one of the holy rollers just stand up and speak out on her husband's behalf?

"Mama Sadie and I wanted you to know that we stand behind our pastor 110 percent." She beamed.

Now Theola knew she was in the wrong building, but she didn't say anything.

"As many of you know, Mama Sadie, as a board member, is in the midst of voting. We expect the results any time now. Shortly after that vote is completed, we will learn the board's decision. The votes will be counted tonight and the results will be available for anyone who's interested. You will be asked to cast your vote in a few days." Most people stood or sat quietly as she spoke.

"Now, I don't need to mention this, but in order to vote you must be a member of Sweetwater Powerhouse of God in good financial standing. We ask that you do not talk to the press. They have been camped out in the parking lot since Sunday school. Are there any questions?"

Theola found it odd that Mama Sadie and Ms. Geraldine had changed their tune. Now all of a sudden they were throwing their support behind her husband. Something wasn't right, and Theola was determined to find out why the tide had suddenly changed.

CHAPTER 27

Pastor Goodlove paced the carpet in his chambers. He was alone like he requested, but his attorneys were right outside the office. The press was still in the parking lot. He had seen two live reports where the press said his fate was being decided.

He had an issue with those words, or with them putting it like that. Pastor Goodlove had long told himself that God was the only one who could judge him. This vote was not going to determine his fate. If Sweetwater's board or members elected to impeach him, he'd be OK. In his own way, he believed he truly was a man of God, and no one but God could determine his fate.

Sure he'd miss the important work he did in the name of Sweetwater PG, but he'd bounce back. He always did. He thought back to the fight he had with his son and grimaced at the memory.

When had things gotten so bad with the Goodlove men? The truth was, he was so wrapped up in what he was doing, he hadn't given much thought to what they were doing. Damien's marriage had fallen apart. Reginald had become a self-doubting shell of a man, and he didn't even know what was going on with Barry.

Pastor Goodlove told himself that if he made it out of this mess, he'd make some changes. He'd make sure he was more appreciative of what he had.

"Don't worry about a thing, Deacon Goodlove. I saw the whole thing with my own two eyes. Your wife hit you first," David, one of the ushers, said.

When the police showed up, Damien didn't know what to think. He wasn't sure who had called the cops over a simple fistfight with his wife, but someone had.

The two officers appeared familiar to him. Some of the ushers had already managed to shuffle Michelle into a nearby room, and a different one was trying to calm him down.

Damien didn't know how he had allowed things to get so out of hand with her. Just like he didn't know how Jazzlyn thought he was going to marry her when she knew the rules before they hooked up.

As the officers approached, Damien tried his best to appear in control.

"Mr. Goodlove, we're looking for your wife, Michelle," one officer said.

"She's in that room there," the usher said. He pointed the officers to the right room and followed behind as they walked over there.

When they escorted Michelle out to a waiting squad car, Damien felt really bad. This was all his fault. If he had been more careful, she wouldn't be in the mess she was in now. He decided he'd bail her out, but it would have to wait until he oversaw the congregation's informational session.

Damien wished he and Michelle hadn't put on such a show on the day the board had planned to vote on his father's future. The board had already made their decision, now it was all up to the parishioners. But he told himself, *What will be will be, and that's all there is to it.*

In the men's restroom, Damien scrutinized his face in the mirror. Michelle had gotten the best of him because he wasn't about to beat up his wife. Hitting women wasn't his style, and he had no idea why he had slapped her.

He used wet paper towels to add pressure to the scratch marks on his face. No matter how much pressure he added, the red and swollen marks were still very prominent. He really didn't want to walk into the packed church with those marks on his face, but he had no choice.

As Damien walked out of the restroom, he ran into one of the ushers who had pulled Michelle off him and into the other room.

"What did the police want with Michelle?" Damien asked. The usher looked around, and then whispered to Damien.

"When they were arresting her, they said something about poisoning and assault charges."

Damien stopped walking.

Michelle? He looked toward the door his wife was escorted out of. *No way! There must be some kind of mistake.* Michelle had been nothing but a good, loving, and caring wife. He had taken advantage of her. He had driven her to physical abuse.

Now, he wondered if he had also driven her to attempted murder.

Reginald still couldn't believe he had quit his job. But he was sick and tired of being treated like he had no value. He was headed to the bank first thing Monday morning. His plans were to withdraw enough money so that he could sit and figure out his next move in peace.

But when he pulled out the checkbook, he realized that if he wrote a check for more than fifty thousand dollars, he was required to have his father's signature. He pulled out some of his father's old documents and began to study the old man's signature.

Not only would he spend Sunday night practicing the old man's signature, but he also planned to write checks out to Candy and Darren. The three of them would have a party, then he'd pack and move.

He would show Ethan Goodlove that his son was no fool. Reginald was so glad that he had finally decided to stand up for himself, that he considered sleeping in the bank's parking lot just to make sure he was there first thing in the morning.

But instead of doing that, he decided to call Candy and tell her about the plans. He needed to make sure she would be on board. After they cashed out, they'd take a trip to Belize or some other exotic location and lounge around like aristocrats.

"Hey, Candy." His voice dropped an octave.

"Pappy, I was just thinking about you. That's why I'm all wet. I was wondering when we were gonna see each other again," she said.

"Well, I'm calling because I need you to do me a favor."

"You got another friend?"

Reginald pulled the phone from his ear and looked at it. He frowned.

"No, nothing like that. Say, what time do you go to work in the morning? I need you to help me with something."

"I'd be happy to help you, Pappy. You just tell me what to do, and how and where to do it," she teased.

Now all he had to do was get Darren on board, and they'd be set.

The more Barry thought about it, the more he felt like a stranger in his own home. He aimlessly walked from the living room to the kitchen to the bedroom. With each step he wondered whether Sissy was watching his every move. After talking with Amy about the tape, he concluded his place must be bugged.

Was his alarm clock a camera? What about the face of the DVD player? Was there a miniature camera in there? Or maybe cameras were hidden in something in his kitchen or bathroom.

Part of the problem was the fact that he just didn't know. He had no idea. Barry strolled into the room he used as a study and glanced around. There were stacks of papers, books, and other things. He glanced up at the ceiling. What if she had a camera installed in the ceiling fan?

Shaking off his paranoia, he sat down at his computer. Since it stayed on 24/7, he only tapped a button to bring it to life.

Barry did a double-take when he glanced at the number of messages in his e-mail's inbox.

"There's no way," he mumbled. "Who gets eight thousand e-mails? What? There's just no way." Barry chuckled as he glanced at the titles of his emails.

"Dog!" He shook his head. "Coward!" He frowned.

"There's got to be some mistake here. I wonder if someone is spamming me." He clicked to open the e-mail titled "Betrayal" and was still confused. He read it again.

> *Dear Barry Goodlove.*
> *I was once married to a vicious snake like yourself. It was so wrong of you to leave that woman at the altar. You and that tramp Amy will pay for what you've done. I don't even know you and I hate you. The woman you jilted may not feel it now, but she's better off without you!*

"This is wild," he said, as he glanced over the other degrading subject titles.

He shook his head. For the first time in days he picked up the phone. The dial tone indicated that he had waiting messages. Barry quickly dialed the number to retrieve his messages.

He nearly fell from the chair when the automated voice said, "You have fifty messages. Your mailbox is currently full."

Barry entered his code to retrieve his messages. The very last one had been left only three minutes before he returned home.

He listened to the voice of a stranger crying.

"Men like you have no idea about the hurt you cause. I hope you and that jezebel burn in hell!"

Barry's eyes widened in confusion.

"What the hell is going on?" he asked the empty room.

The next message said, "I waited outside your church today. You better be glad I don't know what you look like. Your slut wasn't there either. I actually went in and asked for her. People like you don't deserve to breathe. I wonder if your pastor knows what you two did. Hmmm, I might just have to tell him."

"There's got to be some kind of mistake," Barry said. He didn't know what to do, or how to reach Sissy. But he wanted desperately to get to the bottom of this. He knew she was responsible, but he still didn't understand why he had so many hate messages and e-mails.

Barry skimmed through the pages and pages of e-mails until he thought he had found the source message that started off all the hateful responses. When he read the message from someone calling herself "Jilted Lover," he realized it was the same message sent to Amy that was titled "Amy, You Won Finally!"

"Damn you, Sissy," Barry shrieked.

CHAPTER 28

Pastor Goodlove had given lots of thought to the deal he made with some of his church's elders. What was the worst Mama Sadie and her crew could do to him? He'd been thinking about that quite often.

He released a huge sigh of relief when the news was delivered. Sitting at his desk now, he remembered it like it had happened moments ago, instead of days.

The pastor and the attorneys were going over settlement numbers for the three young men who agreed to drop their claims against him when there was a knock at the door.

"The congregation has reached its decision," the board secretary said.

As Pastor Goodlove walked down the hall from his office to the meeting room in the sanctuary, he could hear his heart beating in his ears. He couldn't believe how nervous he was. No one had revealed the board's decision. At the last minute, they decided to seal the results and wait until after the congregation voted. Pastor Goodlove tried the calming exercise he had been practicing.

He paused at the door before swinging it open. The first person he saw was Mama Sadie. She tossed him a wicked smile. Deacon Parker stood.

"The board has decided to impeach you, Pastor Goodlove," he said casually.

The pastor shook his head ever so slightly. He frowned a bit.

"I understand," he said calmly.

Mama Sadie quickly interjected. "It appears that several members of the board have lost confidence in you and your ability to lead this great church. We need to make you aware that you can choose to step down or we can take the vote before the congregation."

"It saddens me to know that Sweetwater's board has no confidence in me. Outside of my personal life, I have an exemplary record. I cannot control the behavior of others, and it amazes me that things have come this far, but I do understand your decision. Now I would like to know how the congregation voted."

It took the members of Sweetwater Powerhouse of God less than two hours to say they not only still had faith in their leader, but they wanted him to remain in charge. This was after their votes had been tallied and several insisted on speaking about the incident.

Although he wasn't required to do so, Pastor Goodlove addressed the members.

"I want to thank each and every one of you for your faith and trust in me. Know that I will not take your trust for granted."

The pastor told himself that the first thing he'd do was figure out a way to get rid of Mama Sadie, her crew, and Deacon Parker.

Before he even had a chance to bask in his victory, Mama Sadie and Ms. Geraldine were in his office.

"Congratulations, Pastor," Mama Sadie sang. Pastor Goodlove didn't respond to that comment.

"Is there something I can do for you ladies?" He looked up from his notes.

"Well, we wanted to discuss the changes we agreed to earlier." Mama Sadie sat down and adjusted herself in the chair across from the pastor's desk.

He looked at Ms. Geraldine, then back at Mama Sadie. He chuckled.

"I don't think there's anything to discuss," he said easily. "Now, if you two don't mind, I have some catching up to do. We are expanding, you know," he said.

Mama Sadie looked at Ms. Geraldine, then back at the pastor. Her eyes were narrow and her teeth gritted.

"I know you're not about to try to go back on your word now, Pastor. We delivered, and we expect you to do the same," Mama Sadie said.

"I'm not doing a damn thing. You don't like it, sue me. Everyone else has!"

Michelle sauntered out of HPD's downtown facility with her attorney in tow. She couldn't believe she had been arrested. They should've tossed that hussy

Jazzlyn behind bars. Not her! As far as she was concerned, she had nothing to be embarrassed about.

Those two should be ashamed. And her attorney warned her to stay away from Jazzlyn and Damien! She would go wherever the hell she wanted, and no one would say she couldn't.

"Remember, 10 A.M. in my office, Mrs. Goodlove. We need to get started on your defense. Your arraignment is next week," he warned.

"Yeah, yeah," Michelle said as she climbed into the cab. She didn't want to ride with him, considering where she was headed. On her way there, she thought of the slip up that led to her arrest.

The day she fought with Damien at the church, she actually thought she was being arrested for whopping his butt, but she soon realized they'd figured out that she was the one who poisoned him.

But her hours spent in jail did give way to a plan. And she was headed to see Deacon Parker right then. Michelle figured that if she teamed up with someone who couldn't stand the Goodlove men, she'd have a better chance at teaching Damien a lesson. After all, just about everyone knew Deacon Parker didn't like the pastor or his sons.

"Oh, Deacon Parker, I was just looking for you," she said seductively as she entered the church.

She noticed his eyes traveling up and down her body. *Damn freak.* Like most men, he had a one-track mind. Michelle offered a fake smile and pulled her bag close to her body.

"You were looking for me? Why?" His eyebrow inched upward. "Thought you were pissed about me going after your father-in-law," he said.

"Deacon Parker, why would that make me mad at

you? I was actually hoping we could team up. Maybe we could both get what we want," she cooed. "Besides, I've heard you're one hundred times better in bed than Damien. So I'm not losing a bit," she smiled.

His eyes lit up at that compliment.

She watched as he sucked it all up. Once she had him smiling, he motioned for her to follow him back to his car.

"Is this some kind of game or something?"

"No, not at all." She smiled.

Deacon Parker opened his car door, but leaned against it instead of getting in. Michelle looked around.

"I think we need to go somewhere private, so we can talk."

"Hmm, OK. That sounds just fine to me," he said.

"I'll follow you. Any place in mind?" she asked before she walked over to her own car.

"Yup, just follow me," he said.

Michelle was so angry and eager for payback that she could hardly think straight.

It didn't take long for them to arrive at the Galleria. They were quickly seated at a booth in the Cheesecake Factory.

"Why don't we have some wine?" she suggested.

"Cool. I'll order a bottle," he said.

"Are you hungry?" Michelle asked.

Deacon Parker excused himself from the table and walked back to the restroom. Michelle had nearly forgotten how she had planned to use him to help destroy her husband. She nearly chickened out on her plan to see Damien suffer, but she snapped out fast enough to smile when their drinks arrived. Deacon

Parker reached for the bottle and filled his glass and hers to the rim.

"I need a man's drink," he said as he guzzled down nearly half of the wine in his first gulp.

"I need someone to help me change leadership at the church. We all know that if pastor screws up again, chances are Damien will be in charge." Michelle shrugged. "I can't imagine Sweetwater in his hands, can you?"

"So what are you proposing?" he asked.

"I say we expose him for all the dirt he's being doing. I've got the pictures and all his other sick mementos. Quite surely, members of this church wouldn't put up with that kind of foolishness.

Michelle looked up at him. He didn't flinch as he swallowed the wine. Deacon Parker stretched his legs.

When his phone rang, she glanced at the bottle that was nearly empty.

"Yeah, I'll be there shortly. I'm discussing business right now," she heard him say.

Deacon Parker hung up the phone and looked at Michelle.

"So you really think I could take over at Sweetwater?" he asked.

"I do, I mean with all that's going on, it's no secret that the Gee man isn't gonna be around forever, and with all this stuff, even if he decides he needs some time off, he sure can't depend on Damien. I think this is our chance to get you in the spotlight."

"Well, what are you suggesting we do?"

"I think the church needs to know what he's been up to. The way he runs around with all those women, at least some of the elders will have issues with that. Think about it. With Pastor's leadership still in question and Damien acting the fool, what better time for you to get out there? You should start by seeing what kind of support there is if any for you to take over, then we move on from there."

"Hmm, I like that."

Michelle leaned in. "But first, I think you should see if some of those women would be willing to speak out against him. We really need to have our stuff together if we're gonna do this."

"Oh, I'm sure I could get a few of them on board," Deacon Parker confirmed.

"Good, let's start with that, then once we have the group together, we'll meet again to talk about what's next."

"OK, I gotta run, but I'm very interested in this plan of yours. I'll start talking with some of the ladies discreetly and let you know what I come up with," he said. Michelle nodded as the deacon excused himself.

Michelle tried to push the thoughts of her arrest out of her mind, but she couldn't. When they read her rights, she knew she couldn't allow Damien to get away with making a fool of her, then jeopardizing her freedom. She wanted revenge, and she was willing to go to great lengths to get it.

CHAPTER 29

For the past three hours Pastor Goodlove had been trying to make some kind of sense out of the church's financial documents. The numbers were just not adding up. It didn't matter what he subtracted or added, the numbers were completely off.

Since Reginald walked out on him, he placed announcements of the job opening on the church's community news board, and on the church's website. He was confident he'd be able to find a good replacement, and he was correct.

In less than one week he had received nearly sixty resumes. And most were very impressive. He refused to call Reginald to straighten out the mess or even try to explain some of the numbers, but he was beside himself the further he dug in. He knew his son was well-educated—the pastor had paid for college for all three of his sons—so it couldn't have been an error.

"I know this isn't what I'm thinking." His brows furrowed. The more he looked at cancelled checks, bank statements, and other financial documents, the more alarmed he became.

"So this boy was stealing from me? All this time, he was right under my nose and robbing me blind?"

Pastor Goodlove felt betrayed. He couldn't believe his son, his own flesh and blood, would steal from him and the church. How would he explain this one to the members of the church? First the impeachment vote, now embezzlement? He shook his head in disbelief.

This had to be some kind of mistake. He decided to call Damien. The pastor wondered if he knew anything about what his brother had been up to.

He reached for the phone, but decided to call the bank instead. Some things just couldn't wait. He wanted to get the facts straight before he made any accusations. Pastor Goodlove only wanted to set up an appointment to discuss the matter with someone. Maybe a personal banker could fix the mess and help make the numbers right, that way he wouldn't have to go accusing Reginald of mismanaging the church's finances.

But what he learned over the phone was even more shocking than the mismatched numbers staring back at him.

Reginald couldn't believe how easy it was to walk away with half a million dollars. He was excited, turned on, and pumped all at once. At first he was going to surprise Candy with a shopping spree, but he decided to hold off on that.

Since he wasn't sure about his next move, he figured he might need to hang on to as much cash as possible.

What if he decided to leave the country? He needed to make sure he had access to quick money.

Darren had been more than willing to help Reginald stick it to the old man. And for his hard work, Reginald gave him fifty thousand dollars. Darren said it was the most money he had ever seen in his life.

Candy was a different story all together. When Reginald tried to talk to her about running away with him, she looked him in the eyes.

"How would we survive?" she asked.

He was baffled at first, not sure if she understood he had enough money for them to survive in a third world country and live like kings for years to come.

"I get paid real good on my job, and I get to meet a lot of interesting people," she told him.

Reginald remembered thinking that was strange. He figured she would want to leave that life behind, but he supposed he was wrong.

It wasn't until the next day when he met Darren for a drink and an update on the old man, that he came up with his plan.

He was taking his money and moving to Belize. There, the U.S. dollar was worth double its value, which meant his five hundred thousand would be a smooth million. Reginald wasn't flashy. He didn't even live well, so the chances of him overdoing it were slim.

One million dollars would be more than enough for him to live on. But he also knew if he stayed in the States and worked for another two years, he might be able to get away with even more. Then he'd have a sweet stash and more than enough to help him make a clean get away.

He was planning an exploratory trip in the coming

days. It was Darren's idea, because he was telling Reginald that's where his family was from, and that he'd planned to send some of his money back home. Reginald quickly decided to take some money down there and start building a dream house. Reginald loved the U.S., but he didn't want to work hard for the rest of his life. And he certainly didn't want to run the risk of getting another boss like the one he just left.

Reginald figured he could build a little business there in Belize, live among the natives, and go undiscovered until, and if, he ever decided to come back to the States again.

Barry nearly ran his car right into the large concrete divider that held the church's neon message board. He could hardly believe his eyes when he looked up and saw the billboard straight ahead.

On the billboard was a picture of him and Amy, the one used for the engagement announcement in the newspaper. The billboard had a message that read: "Find out what they did at backstabbers.com." The billboard had a brief description about how Barry had jilted his fiancée at the altar and announced that he was going to marry Amy instead.

By the time Barry was able to get out of his car, he was one of several people staring up and reading the billboard.

"That Barry was our last hope," he heard a woman say.

"Yeah, you know how those Goodlove men are. Now him too?" the woman tisked. "Bless his poor mother's soul. She must be rolling over in her grave."

"Didn't you get that e-mail about what he did?" the first woman asked.

"No. What e-mail?" That's the moment they looked down and saw Barry standing there.

"Oh-ah, Barry?"

"Ms. Anderson, this is all a huge mistake," Barry tried to explain. He pointed toward the billboard. "You see, this young lady is mad at me."

"And she should be, after what you did. I'd be mad at you, too," a completely different woman said.

Barry sighed. He shook his head and watched as more and more people came over to get a better look at the sign. When a crowd had formed, he cleared his throat loudly.

"OK, people, let me get your attention?" A few people looked down. Some jumped when they realized it was Barry.

"Yes, that is me up there, but you've got to believe me when I say, this is all a huge misunderstanding." Barry felt helpless. Some people appeared to be interested in what he was saying, but most ignored him and started talking about the e-mail.

"Amy, there's a huge billboard right outside of the parking lot," Barry explained to Amy after he left the disgruntled crowd behind. "I was so embarrassed. I called the company that owns it, and they're telling me it's paid up for six months!"

"I cannot believe this. How did this happen? How did you even get mixed up with this woman to begin with?"

"Right now, I just want to figure out a way to get

our pictures off that billboard. The company won't budge," he said.

Barry was thoroughly vexed by the time he hung up with Amy. She told him she'd see if her dad could help. But according to the folks over at Outdoor Images, since the billboard had been paid for six months in advance, it would take an act of Congress to change it.

He sulked into his father's office only to find him just as down and out.

"Gee man, what's wrong with you?" Barry asked. Pastor Goodlove looked up at his son.

"You seen your brother?" he asked.

"Which one? Damien is going through some stuff right now, but you can find him at my place. And I haven't talked to Reginald in a while. Besides, I've got my own problems."

Barry took a seat before his father offered him one.

"What's going on around here?" Barry asked.

Pastor Goodlove motioned for him to close the door. When Barry sat back down, he noticed for the first time just how the stress was taking its toll. He couldn't remember seeing such a dejected look on his father's face.

"Reginald has been embezzling money from the church. He walked out on me the other day and I haven't heard back from him since."

"What? No, not Reginald. I won't believe that."

"It's true. I've got the papers right here. Not only that, I just got off the phone with our banker. In the past two days Reginald has drained more than half a million dollars from the account."

"He wouldn't do a thing like that. You just barely got everyone off your back. Now this?"

Barry sat there thinking about what his father was saying about his brother. Sure, Reginald kept to himself, he didn't socialize much with anyone, but he was not a thief. That much he was sure of.

"Are you sure? I mean, could it be some kind of mistake?"

"I've gone over these numbers more than twenty times, and they're just not adding up. I also remember when he once told me that Theola had been spending something like twenty thousand dollars a month on clothes. Not true. He's been cooking the books." Pastor Goodlove looked up at his son. "The sad thing is, there's no telling how long this has been going on. I found receipts in his office that date back to about three years ago. He was spending thousands on nine hundred numbers and escort services."

Barry rubbed his forehead.

"You're sure about that?" Barry asked.

"Unfortunately, I am."

"So what are you gonna do?"

"Well, I'm gonna call the police and report it. I'm responsible for these people's money. I can't have them thinking I'm not a good steward of their money."

"You can't call the police on your own flesh and blood, Pops. He's your son. We need to find him and figure out what's going on," Barry said.

Considering all that was going on, Barry didn't even feel it was necessary to tell his father what was going on in his own little world.

CHAPTER 30

"Amen, Pastor!" The voices seemed to roar unanimously throughout the sanctuary.

"I know a good, mighty God, huh!" Pastor Goodlove pushed his long, pointed finger toward the ceiling.

"Hallelujah! Pastor, hallelujah!" the crowd responded feverishly.

"He's a mighty, mighty God!" Pastor Goodlove hopped on one leg a few times. His massive frame threatened to topple, but it didn't. Despite his size, the pastor moved like a ballerina on skilled toes.

Mama Sadie started screaming at the top of her lungs. She flung her petite body to the left, threw her arms to the ceiling, and started wailing as she jumped up and down. The Holy Ghost always seemed to visit her during this exact part of Pastor Goodlove's weekly sermon.

"Hello, somebody! I saaaid, I know a mighty, mighty God!" Pastor Goodlove hollered. With his hands now balled into tight fists, he pumped his arms at his sides, shuffled his feet, and moved his massive frame to the left. The organ player's beat matched each step he took, building into a triumphant harmony.

"A mighty, mighty God, and he can help you," he pointed at someone, "and you, and you too, and even me!" With his head flung back and his arms flapping, Pastor Goodlove's chant gave way to song. "I saaaaid, Heeeello, somebody!" the pastor screamed, this time even louder than before.

In the crowd, everyone was sweating, cardboard hand fans with mortuary advertisements quickly swishing back and forth. Soon, most parishioners were up on their feet, humming and dancing along to the contagious beat.

Michelle Goodlove sat at the desk in her office doing nothing in particular. She had a stack of paperwork that needed her attention and several phone calls to return. But on this Wednesday afternoon, her mind was on her marriage that was about to end, this time for good. She was also thinking about what she and Deacon Parker could do to that lousy husband of hers. Once she got the evidence she needed, she'd make sure everyone in the church knew exactly what her husband had been up to over the years. Then she planned to team up with Deacon Parker, then get the information to the holy rollers. She knew it'd only be a matter of time before she destroyed her husband and his reputation.

Damien was supposed to be *the* one, *her* mister right. Unfortunately, he couldn't stop sharing his love with other women. But all of that was now behind her, and she was starting over with a clean slate. Her attorney said that she'd be able to get probation for the assault since she'd never been in trouble before. She told herself it was time to move on.

She refused to be bitter or slumber in self-pity. She'd move on, and she'd do it in a grand way. Out with the old and in with the new—that's what she told herself after she completed the first phase of her new makeover.

Michelle had spent the entire morning at the spa getting the works—a new hairdo with color to match her new makeup and clothes. The clothes were colorful and more revealing and sexy than her old wardrobe—stuff she'd never wear when she was with Damien.

She'd become the new and improved Michelle, and when Damien laid eyes on her again, he'd regret having used her heart as a doormat to rub his feet and stomping all over her feelings. These were her thoughts as the phone rang. Michelle considered not picking up at all, but too many people had seen her stroll into the office, so pretending she was out would've been useless.

"This is Mrs. Goodlove," she said cheerfully.

"Yes, Mrs. Goodlove, this is Bridgett, the nurse from Dr. Adams's office. Your blood work has come in, and the doctor needs to see you immediately to discuss the results."

"Ah, can't you tell me over the phone? Just call a prescription in to the pharmacy if I need one? I mean, what, do I have cancer or something?" she asked jokingly.

"Mrs. Goodlove, we didn't test you for cancer, but the doctor would like to see you as soon as possible."

Michelle glanced at the calendar on her desk.

"How about tomorrow, Thursday, at three thirty?" she asked.

"How about four thirty today? Dr. Adams' last appointment is at three forty-five. She could see you at four fifteen or four thirty," the nurse said.

"Oh, that shoe sale at Saks starts at five, and I have got to be there the minute they open the doors," Michelle said.

"Mrs. Goodlove, Dr. Adams only needs fifteen minutes of your time. You can go to the sale after your appointment."

"Emph, I guess you're right. After all, my health is far more important than 75 percent off designer brand shoes, right? I'll be there at four fifteen," Michelle said.

After spending most of the morning re-inventing herself at the salon/spa, she really didn't need to leave work early, but she told herself this was a legitimate excuse. Well, not the sale part, but definitely the doctor's appointment.

Two hours after the initial call, Michelle sat waiting in Dr. Adams's office. She was glad they didn't place her in an exam room, because that meant she'd be out quickly. As far as Michelle was concerned, the good doctor had ten minutes to tell her the diagnosis, write a prescription, and send her on her way. If she was lucky, she'd be able to drop off the prescription at CVS, rush to the shoe sale, and pick up her medicine on her way back home.

Dr. Adams walked in and pulled the door closed behind her.

"Mrs. Goodlove, how are you feeling today?" she asked.

"I'm good, thanks for asking. Now what is this

about? I hope I don't have another urinary tract infection. Those things are so worrisome," Michelle said. She noticed Dr. Adams looking through her medical file and jotting down notes as she spoke, so she quickly stopped talking. "So, what is it doc?"

Dr. Adams closed the file and folded her hands on top of it.

"There really is no easy way to say this, Mrs. Goodlove."

Michelle's eyebrows inched upward. She felt her heartbeat begin to race, and her palms begin to moisten. Still, she controlled her breathing. How bad could it be? Suddenly, Dr. Adams got up from her chair and walked around her desk to be at Michelle's side.

"Your blood work has come back abnormal. You are aware that we performed an HIV test? And, well, you've tested positive. We will of course administer another test just to be sure, but your initial results did come back positive."

Michelle swallowed hard and looked Dr. Adams square in the eyes. She blinked back tears that were beginning to sting as they pooled in her eyes. She swallowed again. Michelle wanted to be anywhere but there.

"Mrs. Goodlove? We will test again. But in the meantime, I wanted to make sure you are aware that HIV is the virus that causes AIDS. Many people are able to live long, productive years with HIV and even full-blown AIDS. Please know we have counselors who specialize in this sort of thing. You are not alone. What we'd like to do, is send you back to the lab first thing in the morning. We'll retest, and then wait two weeks for those results." Dr. Adams paused, and then continued. "Now, I know this won't be easy, but in the meantime, I need you to sit here and put together a list of the names of all of your sexual partners from the past five years." Dr. Adams touched Michelle's shoulder.

"I know this is difficult, but you can survive this."

"I'm married. I've only had one sexual partner in the last five years," she said with quivering lips. Michelle squeezed her eyes shut. She hesitated for a moment, and then with shaky fingers, she touched Dr. Adams's hand. "I am HIV positive?" Her eyes snapped open.

"Yes. Yes, that's what the results show," Dr .Adams said.

CHAPTER 31

The more time that passed, the more devastating the church's financial situation appeared to be. Pastor Goodlove couldn't believe the state of his finances. He felt violated, like some stranger had come in and gone through all of his personal information.

Sweetwater wasn't about to go bankrupt anytime soon, but just knowing that a thief was so close, and he had no idea, made him feel sick to his stomach.

His congregation had already forgiven the mess Maurice and the others started. The last thing he wanted to do was to give them something else to criticize him about.

As Pastor Goodlove sat at his desk, there was a knock at the door. His wife stuck her head in.

"You're alone. I'm glad," she said.

"What is it, Theola?"

Dressed in a leopard-printed skintight bodysuit and thigh high boots, she walked in with a thick folder.

"You have got to see what I have in here!" she squealed.

"Not now, Theola. I've got some things I'm working on, and I really need to concentrate." Theola shook her head.

"No, you need to hear this. This could change a lot of things around here. I knew something was going on, and I've finally gotten to the bottom of it."

Pastor Goodlove looked up at his wife.

"OK, you have fifteen minutes, then I'm gonna have to get back to work. Now what is it?"

"You will never guess who was behind all of that mess with the lawsuits," Theola said. Her eyes lit up when she slammed the folder down in front of her husband. He slowly flipped it open.

"What is all of this?"

"I'm glad you asked. I hired a private investigator to look into this whole mess. And you'll never begin to guess who was behind it all!"

"Mama Sadie?" Pastor Goodlove slowly mumbled.

"That's right. That old, mean bitch was behind it all. Maurice was one of her foster children. It's all in here. The plan was for him to entice you. He was going to make a pass at you then cry sexual harassment. He was supposed to trick you into giving him as much money as he could before threatening with a lawsuit that they just knew you'd agree to settle out of court. Then, they were gonna try to get you kicked out as pastor. The plan was to put Deacon Parker in charge. Apparently, Deacon Parker and Mama Sadie's daughter had something going on back in the day."

Pastor Goodlove looked at his wife, then back at the contents in the folder.

"This can't be real," he said. Pastor Goodlove had thrown money at the problem, figuring he'd avoid public embarrassment, but never once did he consider the boy had been out to get him in the first place. He was silent as he flipped through the information in the folder.

"This can't be real," he repeated.

"Oh, it's real all right, and it's all in there for you to see."

"But how did you get all of this? I know you hired someone, but how did he find out all of this information?"

"Everybody talks to somebody. It's just a matter of finding out who your nemesis is talking to. I knew I didn't like that bitch. I knew it, I knew it! Always judging somebody, telling other people they aren't good enough, when all along she was plotting to get you out of here!"

"But why?" Pastor Goodlove asked, not really addressing the question to Theola.

"Keep reading. It seems that the old bag has a gambling habit that's out of control!"

"What?"

"Yeah, it's all in there. Read it. Oooh, what are we gonna do to her? Let's clown her in front of the whole church. Let's get her, Deacon Parker, Ms. Geraldine, and the rest of those no good holy rollers!"

For a while longer Pastor Goodlove sat flipping through the folder. Every detail seemed more interesting than the one before. He couldn't believe what his eyes were taking in.

"So they had this elaborate plan to get control of the church?"

"Yes, because once Deacon Parker was in control,

she'd have her hands on the purse strings. Then I guarantee you that Sweetwater would've been a thing of the past. She would've gotten her hands on the money and all of it would've gone straight to the casino!"

Theola threw her head back and laughed. She laughed hearty and hard.

"OK, wait a second here," Pastor Goodlove said.

"No, I want to go find them now. You know they're probably getting ready for Bible study. I want them to know that we know! I want them out of this church right this minute!"

"I want you to calm down, Theola!"

"Calm down? No, I want them out. I've given you all the proof you need. You now know that this was a set-up all along. They purposely tried to drag your name through the mud and made you look bad. I say we deal with them quickly and publicly." Pastor Goodlove held up his hand.

"I'm glad you got this, Theola. But it ends here. We're going to stop this here and now."

"What? What do you mean end it here and now? They tried to destroy you, us. They can't stand me. I want them to be dealt with!"

"I know, Theola. I know you do. But I want you to read my lips. I want you to understand what I'm telling you. We will not do a single thing to Mama Sadie, Ms. Geraldine, or anyone else."

"What? How come? We've finally got those old hags," Theola cried. The pastor looked at his wife.

"I'm tired, I'm done. We're going to forgive and forget. We're starting a new day here at Sweetwater, and I want to put all of this foolishness behind us as we look toward expanding. I don't want us to take none of this mess with us. Understand?" Pastor Goodlove looked down at the folder again.

"If Jesus could forgive those who plotted against him, I'm sure we could forgive Mama Sadie and her crew," he said.

Theola pouted, but eventually she nodded her head in agreement with her husband.

Damien sat at the phone staring at it as if he could erase the last phone call he received from his wife. He was still speechless after Michelle's call.

HIV positive? He was not expecting that at all. When he sat and tried to think of where he could've possibly gotten the disease, so many names flashed across his mind that he could barely think straight.

One or more of those one night stands, romps in the office, in the backseats of cars, or in parks late at night had left him with the big disease with the little name.

And what was worse, he had passed it along to his wife. He had been willing to forgive her for the poisoning incident, but now it was he who needed forgiveness. He had no idea what he was going to do. The first thing he needed to do was go get tested. He knew he needed to call some of the women he'd been sleeping around with.

It was all his fault, and he knew it. He didn't know what to say or what to do. He picked up the phone and called for a doctor's appointment. Damien knew he'd be sick until he had the test and got the results.

He also decided he'd wait until after the results before he started making calls and confessions.

* * *

Reginald's initial trip to Belize was enough to convince him to move immediately. He didn't want to run the risk of getting in trouble with his father or anyone else. After all, he had taken quite a bit of money. He knew that his father wasn't the type of man to just sit back and say he lost. There was no telling what the Gee man had planned for him once he found out about the money.

Reginald wasn't too worried about the church, though. He knew Sweetwater would be just fine. That money would be replaced in less than six months. His father may as well be known as the holy hustler as far as he was concerned. The way he hustled money from the congregation was nothing less than amazing. And the fact that they gave and gave cheerfully never seemed to stop amazing him.

It took Reginald three days to close out all his business in the States. When Candy refused to quit her job, he decided he didn't want to waste any more time or money on her. And although he and Darren had gotten close, he felt it best not to involve him in his plans to leave the country.

The two-hour flight to Belize was nearly over. From his window seat, Reginald's eyes took in miles and miles of greenery as the plane began to make its descent. Reginald struggled to contain his excitement. When the flight attendant's accented voice rang through the intercom, Reginald glanced around the cabin and smiled.

"Welcome to Belize," he mocked, imitating the flight attendant.

He wanted to do everything—visit the Keys and go

to Crooked Tree, one of the world's best cashew farms. He planned to go clubbing and check out some Belizean women.

Reginald wasn't the least bit concerned about restarting his life and moving to the small country. He glanced out the window again. If all went well, he'd set up his own escort business for tourists.

When the seatbelt light went out, the other passengers bolted from their seats. Reginald remained seated and waited for the crowd to leave the plane.

At the small airport, he gathered his bags, cleared customs, and found his driver holding a name card. He followed the man to a waiting car.

"You staying at the Princess, huh?" The driver glanced at Reginald through the rearview mirror.

"Yes, I am, but not for long. My house should be ready soon, out in Eight Mile," Reginald confirmed.

"Excellent choice. How about I drop you at the hotel, you freshen up, change, and I come back say, in about two hours, then we go meet Binky? First you talk business, then we party. Good?"

"That's all good, Melvin. That's all good," Reginald said.

As they spoke, Reginald focused on the narrow streets. He couldn't believe how the drivers recklessly passed each other on the road. In the center of Belize City, he gazed at the large drawbridge where tons of boats were docked. The locals gathered to buy fish fresh from the boats. The houses on nearby streets were mostly made of wood, and were of various shapes and sizes. All were painted in an array of bright colors.

After his exploratory trip around Belize City, he used his cell phone to make calls and set up a few business meetings. Binky would help organize the business and provide models for him to interview.

When they pulled up to the modern hotel that served as a casino and a movie theatre, Melvin quickly jumped out of the car. He opened Reginald's door first, then raced to the trunk.

"Wow, it's so hot here." Reginald used his hand to wipe a thin line of perspiration from his forehead.

"It is." Melvin nodded. "So you'll want to dress comfortably for tonight."

Three hours later, Melvin pulled up to a house more elaborate than any Reginald had seen since he arrived.

"This is like something you'd see in the States," Reginald said.

"Yeah. How do you say in the States . . . big time!" He flicked his hands.

"Big time?" Reginald chuckled. "So, even Belize is home to some big-timers." Reginald glanced around the sprawling property.

Binky was a big man, who appeared to indulge in everything pleasurable—expensive clothes, good food, and lavish jewelry. His time was valuable and he moved like a man who never had enough of it to spare.

"Reginald. Welcome! Welcome." he cheered, as Reginald and the driver walked through the doors. "Your flight was enjoyable?"

"Yeah, it was cool," Reginald confirmed. He glanced around the room. The great room had two floor-to-ceiling glass windows. Swags framed them both, and they were surrounded by textured walls. The furniture was all leather and matched the wall's navy pattern.

"I live just as comfortably here as I would in the States," Binky commented. "I designed and decorated this myself."

"It's nice," Reginald said.

"Come. We go out to the veranda. There we talk, drink rum, and eat panades."

Reginald followed Binky's wide frame out to a net-enclosed veranda. It ran along the length of the entire house.

"I give you the ladies, you get everything organized. When you ready, I help spread the word about the new business." Binky leaned forward. "The ladies here are beautiful. Smart businessmen like yourself find ways to turn such beauty into great wealth, if they so desire."

"That'll work," Reginald said. "That'll work."

When Amy walked into Barry's apartment, the smile had returned to her face. He hadn't seen it in quite some time.

"What gives?" he asked immediately.

"My daddy has fixed it all!" she screamed.

"What do you mean?" Barry didn't want to get too excited too fast.

"He took care of everything. The billboard is gone, and there won't be any more e-mails. He even had someone talk to Sissy. It's all over!"

"But how?" Barry wanted to know. He shook his head in disbelief.

"That's the thing about my daddy. He's the greatest man to walk the earth. He always fixes everything. I knew he would and he did. So now we can move forward with the plans for our wedding. We don't have to worry about any more distractions," Amy said.

Barry knew he should've been thrilled by her news. It was like his prayers were answered, but still he didn't feel quite right about what Amy was saying.

Then there was the way she was going on and on about what a great man her father was. He felt a ping of jealousy, but he told himself he shouldn't feel that way. Instead, he wanted to focus on this blessing and move forward.

Barry had learned a valuable lesson. He learned that his walk was a continuous one. He knew he needed to work a little harder.

Amy jumped into Barry's arms and wrapped her arms around his neck. She squeezed tightly.

"I say, we move the wedding up before that crazy woman or anyone else has a chance to try to prevent it again."

"I think you may be on to something there. I really do." Although he was basking in the good news with Amy, something told Barry that it wasn't over between him and Sissy. He didn't care how powerful Mr. Blackwell was, there was no telling what a woman scorned was capable of.

About the Author

P.L. Wilson is an award-winning journalist who spent years as a TV news reporter. She lives in Houston, where she currently works at a local radio station in the news department. P.L. is also a freelance writer for the *Houston Defender*, Houston's oldest black newspaper. She is a member of the National Association of Black Journalists and its Houston chapter. She is currently working on her next novel, the sequel to *Holy Hustler*.